A narrator from a post apocalyptic world introduces the work of a newly discovered author, SD Downs, in a world where the ever decreasing remaining books are the last form of passive entertainment left for Humanity. As well as their introduction to the first new author in a hundred years, they reveal snippets of how and why the world ended, what state it is in now and how they came to find his previously unpublished work.

Lost in the Apocalypse

An Introduction to SD Downs

First published in Great Britain in 2020.

A CIP catalogue record for this book is (probably?)
available from the British Library

Dedicated to my father David Downs who passed on his love of reading to me and thus is responsible for all of this. It's all his fault, if you've got any problems with it, take it up with him.

Also, big shout outs to:
my wife (the official unofficial editor)
children (inspiration and illustration)
university friends (ideas and drunken conversation)
school friends (I may have stolen some of your names)
and teachers (I'm so sorry about my hand writing and spelling)

I'm sorry if I have ever harassed you in the past with my poor attempts at writing, I promise I'll stop now. Honest.

No chair legs were used in the making of this book. Was it a chair leg or a table leg? I'm so sorry Amanda.

Contents

1

I've spent many of the last few
months researching SD Downs and his
work and now I am finally ready to
start presenting my findings. Many
of the stories that you are about to
read come directly from his own
computer. I have more, from before
he had a computer and from after,
but I thought I would start with
these.

I am sitting at his computer right
now, writing this. It's an old Mac
from about 2012, which is kind of
funny because as well as his writing
the computer also has a bunch of
other stuff on it including a movie
titled "2012" which is about the end
of the world. The movie is both
hilariously inaccurate and
devastatingly true at the same time.

If you're reading this you'll
probably understand why I find an
old movie about the end of the world
so funny. Or possibly not. I find
other people often think that what

I'm thinking is odd; which isn't odd because I find almost everyone else I've met to be very odd. Though I haven't met many people.

I have traveled across much of what's left of the globe (yes, the world is a globe shape, all you flat Earthers are just wrong) doing my research but now I am sat here in the garage of his last house. This is where it all started for me, where it all ended for him and where I intend to finish it.

I found the old Mac wrapped in a blanket on the floor in here along with all its wires and gubbins. His house is all covered in solar panels and he has three different kinds of windmill in his garden but nothing in the house works, which is totally to be expected. The big battery in the garage however, still had a blinking light on it when I found it, and the light worked when I flicked the switch.

I'm guessing he must have set it all up after. I'm not really guessing, nothing from before works so obviously this must have been set up afterwards. I guess my "guessing" is that it was him that did it. Anyhow there is power in the garage, probably the only place there is in a hundred mile radius, so when I found the computer I plugged it into the sole power socket and bugger me if it didn't just work.

There was an old desk and chair in here too so I've kind of set myself up a nice little office space. I even have a bookcase and a battered old metal filing cabinet; and a rug. I haven't plugged in any other electrical appliances, there are some in the house, but I didn't want to risk them breaking what was currently working.

Anyway, this is probably the cosiest set up I've had, my little office with a working light, a comfy desk chair and a fully working computer. I'm getting off topic, you don't need to know about me and anyone who might read this already knows all about about what happened and why nothing works, all that stuff is boring. I'm here to tell you about SD Downs. SD Downs wasn't boring, he led a very good life and he left

behind some excellent stories. Some
of which might be true, to some
extent, but I think most are just
made up. Probably.

The first story that I am going to
share is called "Dead Bird". I

know. Doesn't sound great does it?
I guess even SD Downs knew that
because he changed the title later
to "Lucky 5" but I still think of it
as "Dead Bird". If I'm honest, it
isn't his best work ever, but it is
still good.

The reason I'm starting with "Dead
Bird" is that it's the earliest work
of his that I can find on the Mac.
It's from the file called "Old PC
Stuff" which is full of stuff from
his old computer. Pretty obvious
that really.

That file has a bunch of old
photographs, scans from real paper
printed photographs not digital
ones. I think in the oldest
pictures, where he looks youngest,
they show him at University. There
are also some of his wife when she
was still his girlfriend (including
a rather racey one where she's just
in her bra) and his university
friends before you get to wedding
photographs and then Hungary.

For anyone out there reading this
who was born after, "Hungary" is the
name of a "country". Basically

before it happened all of the land was divided up into smaller bits that were "countries", they didn't seem to do it with the sea just the land. They each had a name, some spoke different languages and they all tried to keep all their stuff in their country whilst trying to get the good stuff from other countries into their country, to make their country be the one that had most stuff.

The countries would encourage people who had lots of stuff to come to their country, with all their stuff. They hated it if anyone with not very much stuff tried to come into their country. They were frightened those people would try and take stuff from the people that already lived there, leaving them with less stuff. It's kind of confusing but it's just what they did before.

As far as I can figure out that's the reason for what happened. Eventually several of the countries got all of the "stuff" and the people in the countries that didn't have any stuff either left those countries or died. When there were

just three or four countries left
they stopped letting people move
between the countries so the stuff
all stayed in one country.

Then some people within each country
started to collect together as much
stuff as they could from everybody
else in that country until most of
the stuff was owned by just a few
people. That was when it really got
started. The end. Or the beginning
of the end. Or maybe I mean the end
of the beginning of the end and the
real start of the end began. I'm
getting off track again.

SD Downs went to Loughborough
University, in England (another
"country") where he studied to
become a librarian, That's the job
of looking after books. He played
lots of different sports, made a few
short term friends and started
getting his stories published. I
have those stories in my filing
cabinet, they were serialised in
"The Elvyn Richards News" magazine.
One of them even won a short story
competition held by the magazine.
They were formative works, really
only first drafts of ideas when

compared to his later work.

As well as the stories and photographs in "Old PC Stuff" there were some music files and a beginning of a journal that only lasts a few months during the beginning of his final year in Hungary. For some reason, after spending three years at Loughborough University learning how to be a librarian SD Downs then moved to Hungary and became a teacher. He spent two years teaching the English language to people in Hungary who didn't know how to speak English. Like I said some of the countries had their own languages and they didn't speak English so he taught them.

SD Downs wrote "Dead Bird" during his first year teaching, and it's about a teacher, which makes sense. It could be true, although the main character doesn't come across as very SD Downs-y to me. There are some true bits in it (he explains in his introduction) and he built a story around them.

I've waffled on long enough, you're

not here for me, time to read some
classic SD Downs. (Like I said: not
his best, but still good and a nice
taste of what he's like.)

Lucky 5

(Dead Bird)
Word Count: 2466

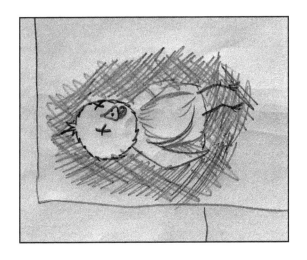

By SD Downs

Kiskunhalas 2020

Intro

I wrote this short story in 2020, I was living in Hungary teaching English at the time having just finished university. I wouldn't have known the word back then, but it is clear to me reading it now that the main protagonist is, at the very least, a bit Autistic. It was originally titled "Dead Bird" and is part of a series of short stories that I wrote that all contained a death within them. This was the first in the series and the death has already happened by the time the story starts, it was nothing to do with the protagonist but still, he has to deal with it. In his own, slightly odd, way.

There was this dead bird on the path on my route to work. It was just lying there, kind of dead looking... It was small, but no baby. Its head was kind of crooked. It lay on the path, on its back looking off to the left and up a little bit. I thought it must have been looking at my ear as I passed by it.

I don't know why a dead bird would want to look at my left ear, I had cleaned it that morning in the shower; I had held the shower head so that it sprayed water right into my ear and after the shower I had used one of those cotton buds, twirling it around in my ear, going as deep as I dared. Those cotton buds are strange; it always tells you on the little pot that they come in that you must not put them in your ears. But that is the only reason I know to buy them. The companies must just be covering themselves in case dumb people shove one of the little ear buds right into their ear perforating their eardrum and poking a hole into their brain. Or something. With the warning there the companies can say, "We recommended that they didn't do that" and they would not get into any trouble. "They were not using it for our products intended purpose" they would say. I would love to be a lawyer or the judge in that case. I would ask him right back "And just what is the intended purpose of your product?" And the guy would just look guilty, maybe pull on his collar a bit, wipe the sweat from his brow and say whatever lie his company had told him to. But everybody knows that those little cotton buds are for cleaning your ears, whatever other uses there may be for them, cleaning ears is what they are for.

And cleaning my ears is exactly what I had used cotton buds for that morning before the dead bird started looking at me. My ears were so clean it must have been looking at something else. I don't have dandruff either; I had used an antidandruff shampoo in that shower this morning. I guess it was just staring where its eyes were letting it because it was dead and couldn't do much about moving them.

So, Yeah! I walked past this dead bird on this particular day. And it stared at my ear and I stared at its small body, noticing a small dent in the neck of the poor creature. I work at this Primary School. It is painted a cream colour, and all the woodwork is brown. The metal gates are brown too. The gates look strange, but good; they are like two old-fashioned radiators, big thick tubular ones, that have been stretched out to become gates.

The School building is a large 'U' shape, when you have walked through the gate you are standing inside the U. I walked through the gate, inside the U, and then past the reception man nodding my head and pretending to mumble some sort of good wish. Then I walked up the sweeping staircase and into the sanctity of the staff room, ignoring the giggling group of twelve-year-old girls I had to walk past at the top of the stairs. I always get there early. It is my way of allowing some preparation time, time when my head can get used to the idea of being at work. I can sit in the staff room and look about a bit, see what's going on. That's a lie. I just sit in one of the comfy chairs and daydream. Eventually my mentor teacher, I work in Hungary as an English teacher so I suppose they feel the need to train me a little, comes in and speaks to me. We sit there and hold a little conversation just like two little friends any where in any English speaking country.

Yeah! So, then I teach. But I am thinking of this dead bird that I've seen. I have a really clear picture in my head of it lying on the path. It's not just a photo from this morning though; it's a real close up photo now, like I had crouched down and got really close to it. I didn't though, and I hadn't. I don't know how our minds can do things like that. I suppose they are just like really good computers and can just do these things. I don't understand computers either, although I can work with them, like I can work with my brain.

The next day when it was still there, I did crouch right down, and I had a really good look at it. Well, in my mind. I didn't physically go any closer at all. In a way I was scared of it. It was only a small bird, but it was dead, and it had been there for at least a day now. That means even if being dead doesn't make you dirty it must be dirty now. Anything would be dirty if you just left it lying on the path like that. And it had been left there, because there it was, still there on my way to work.

Strange, I thought, that I hadn't looked at it on my way home from work the other day. Today I will make sure to have a look at it on my way home. With this thought in my head I could carry on walking. I must have looked pretty silly standing still and looking at the floor. Even weirder if they could see what it was that I was looking at. But what did I

care? I would never know what they thought, and I

didn't care. I carried on, and walked to my radiator

gates in front of my 'U' shaped school to my safe staff

room and the comfortable chair that awaited me.

So, again, I taught. But I thought of that dead

bird. All day it seemed I thought of that poor dead

bird. It was small but it was not a baby, just a small,

little bird. A Starling? I didn't know, I don't know

anything about birds. I don't know what their names

are or what they do. Birds are just birds. And this

one was small and also dead. Did I mention that it

was black? Black with a dark brown tummy. Well

some of the feathers there were a little brown.

All day I thought of that little dead black and

brown bird. But again when I walked home I forgot about it. I must have walked within 1 metre of the dead animal, thinking about it as I forgot to look at it again.

Once at home, a small flat which I shared with two other tenants a bedroom each, one kitchen, one bathroom and a toilet, I again remembered the little creature. Anything could have happened to it during the day. Anyone could have stood upon it, I myself could have stepped on it as I walked home, or any old cat could have taken it away, anything. Anything. I decided that I must see it at least one last time. So, I set out on a journey to the shops, my sole purpose was really just to see that little dead bird. Normally my walk to the shops would not take me past the place where the dead bird lay, but now it would and I would see that little dead bird.

I was a little excited as I prepared to leave the flat, not for work this time but for a gentle stroll to a couple of the shops, maybe pick up something for dinner. But most exciting of all I would see my little dead bird again. I decided that I should introduce myself to it. It seemed rude to look at it for a third time and not introduce myself. OK, so the bird hadn't talked to me either but one must take the initiative in these situations. Besides, the little bird was dead after all.

With excitement building in my stomach, like a child who is about to start the journey for its first day at school, I opened my front door. A little apprehensive, but also excited knowing that what lay before me could only be a good thing. But still… A little scared.

I marched down the hallway of my building out the front door turning left and along the path that would take me to the little dead bird. As I walked passed the house at the end of the street that they had been building ever since I was here, but that they were never going to finish, I imagined that people who saw me must have thought 'there is a man with a job to do' as I apparently struck boldly towards my target. But inside I was beginning to have doubts. Maybe I hadn't looked at the bird on the way home because it was no longer there. After all anything could have happened to it. There had been men weeding the dirt in the cracks in the pavement. They had been around the corner from my dead bird, but that had been in the morning. Surely they would have seen my bird and taken him away.

For the first time my stride faltered, just a little, as the thought struck me. But I strode on determined that whatever would be would, quite simply, be. As I approached the stretch of path on which my dead little bird was lain I thought something must have happened to the little chappie. When I was only 15 metres from the spot, I was certain that it wouldn't be there, I held my eyes high. I looked straight forward not daring to see if I could spot the black smudge in the distance that would materialize as a dead bird. I marched thus until I was standing right at the spot. Then I stopped still. Pausing, still looking forward I didn't move. Maybe two seconds passed as I plucked up the courage to look down and... There he was! Oh great relief. He was there. My little bird. Still in one piece. Exactly as I had seen him last time that very morning.

Relief flooded through me. I was extremely happy. A big grin must have spread across my face; an old lady with a tattered, dirty shopping bag gave me a queer look as she passed me by. I noticed that after she had gone past me she stopped and looked back at me for a few seconds. I tried to compose myself under her inspection. I stood up straight. Looked up and nodded in her direction and then continued to walk on my way to the shops.

I was so relieved, first at the bird actually still being there, and then at getting out of the situation with the old woman that I had completely forgotten my intentions to introduce myself to the small dead bird. At first I was shocked at how rude I must seem. Then I was a little scared at what the consequences might be. Then I thought about how bad I would feel if I was that bird. My shopping was a shambles; my frame of mind forbade me to do anything correctly. I picked up the wrong foods, gave the woman the wrong coins and said the wrong words. My mind was focused on the pain in my stomach that signified I had done something to hurt another being's feelings.

Carrying my little plastic bag of wrong food I started the little trek home. I mustn't forget the bird. I mustn't forget the bird. I mustn't forget the bird. At one level my mind just continued repeating those sentiments maybe a thousand times as I walked, while at another level I alternately felt embarrassed for not introducing myself, and then wondered if it was possible to introduce oneself on a fourth encounter. Eventually I decided it would have to be possible because a fourth encounter introduction was the best that I could do now. As I reached this decision I also reached the spot where my little dead bird was, or where he had been, for he certainly was not there now.

I felt a great deal of sadness. Certain that it was my rudeness that had made that little dead bird go away. I shuffled the rest of the way home and dumped my plastic bag of wrong food on the kitchen table not even bothering to unpack it. It could melt and rot for all I cared. I felt terrible. I just kept trying to imagine how that bird must have felt. It was awful. If I was really rude I wouldn't have given it a second thought, but I was not that rude, and I felt terrible.

I lay awake that night feeling sad. I didn't eat in the morning, but left early on my journey to school.

I hadn't expected the bird to be back in its spot but when I reached it, and it really still wasn't there I had fresh strong waves of guilt and sadness. I stood at the spot for a while; for me it was like the scene of a crime. A crime that I had committed and was yet to be punished for. How sorry I was. After a while two little old ladies walked past me and blatantly stared at me. I ignored them and stood in a quiet humble sort of way. As a third old lady walked by staring at me I started a little prayer for my dead little lost bird, ignoring the foreign words she mumbled to herself quietly as if I wouldn't hear it because I was strange and foreign. I prayed. It was after all dead, and that's when you need prayers the most, when you are dead. I prayed that it was in a better place and that it had friends. I even half prayed that one day when I was dead I could meet it and explain how sorry I was, maybe go to a bar and buy it a drink. I felt in some way that we would certainly become good friends and laugh about how I never introduced myself until our fifth meeting and by then we were both dead.

I was gone by the time the fourth old lady passed by. Four always has been my unlucky number. And five, well five has become my lucky number; I'm sure five will be good to me.

2

Well, there you go. You have met SD Downs, what did you think? Not bad huh? Don't worry, it gets much better, that was just a taster but I kind of like that one anyway. The next one is similar but after that they start to get bigger and better.

As far as I can tell SD Downs really enjoyed living in Kiskunhalas, during his first year in Hungary, but he did write a lot of stories about dead animals or death in general while he was there. I guess there were a lot of dead animals around at the time. You have to remember that before the humans really kicked off with "The End" the world was starting to crumble around them.

While all the people were concentrating on getting "the stuff" they became completely blind to where the stuff came from. Some of the stuff came from inside the earth, so as they emptied out the inside of the earth big holes were left underground. Sometime, around when SD Downs was in Hungary, some of the holes started to get so big that what was above them collapsed into them.

It's pretty obvious really, you can see them all around today. The "stuff" must have been pretty amazing to distract the people from seeing it happen. But that's what all the big holes around us are, places where the biggest houses with the most stuff in them used to be.

I've been down more than my fair share of holes, as I'm sure you have, and to be honest I'm not that impressed with any of the stuff I've found down there. Most of it is broken now and the rest doesn't seem to be much use. If it wasn't for the food and drinks in cans it wouldn't be worth bothering with. Some of that food and drink is amazing though, so down we all go, no matter how dangerous it might be. Root beer is my favourite but absolutely, totally the rarest.

Imagine spending your life filling

your massive home with loads of stuff until it becomes so heavy with stuff and the hole under your house gets so big that your house (and all your stuff) falls into the hole and kills you. The holes had started by Kiskunhalas 2020 but nobody was really noticing them. They were only small single home ones at that time. They sometimes wrote about them in newspapers but that was all. They described them as "anomalies" and how they happened was unknown. No thought at all about how to stop them. Stupid.

As well as the digging and the holes they had to do a lot of burning to make the stuff and move it about and that was what started making the air like it is today. As we all know, that can kill things. Hence all the dead animals that SD Downs must have been seeing and why he wrote about them. I guess that they had only just started in Kiskunhalas 2020 and that was why he found them so interesting.

There must have been enough of them and SD Downs found them interesting enough that the next story I'm going

to share with you, also from
Kiskunhalas 2020, is also about a
dead animal. This one is called
"Dead Mouse".

Now, this one is a bit odd because
it is set in Szentes (I'm pretty
sure, from my research) which is the
place he lived during his second
year in Hungary but he wrote it
during his first year while he was
living in Kiskunhalas. To increase
the odd the story after this one was
written while he lived in Szentes
but is set in Kiskunhalas. Or maybe
that just evens it out.

That's getting ahead of myself, so
first, here's Dead Mouse:

DEAD MOUSE

Word Count: 1662

By SD Downs

Kiskunhalas 2020

Intro

I wrote "Dead Mouse" whilst living in Kiskunhalas but it is set in a house I know in Szentes. It is part of a series of short stories that all feature a death. In "Dead Mouse" the death has already occurred before the story starts and while the protagonist isn't responsible for the death directly it is connected to them via where it occurred and by what caused the death. I'm not sure why it came out in the voice of a child but I felt that it definitely had and in rewrites I cemented that into the story.

There is a dead mouse. It is outside my house. Well, it's not really my house (because I am only a seven year old girl) but it is the house that I live in. My home. Anyway, about this mouse, it's dead, and outside, my mouse. Last night I came home and, although it was dark, I could swear that there was no mouse. This morning I got out of bed, washed, dressed and went out and saw the mouse. It was dead when I saw it and it is still dead now. And it's outside my house. You may think that I am pressing too hard on this point (that's something my Mum always says, if I want something and I keep asking her for it, she says "You're pressing too hard, you had better be careful, or something will break!") but it is a DEAD mouse and it is outside MY house. Not yours, or his or hers, mine.

A dead mouse outside my house. It sounds a little poetic. I suppose that is because it rhymes, but it's not a nice thing, like rhymes normally are. Normally rhymes and poems are about beautiful things like flowers and birds and lovely people. But then I suppose not all people are lovely, there can be horrid people too. Stacy, at school, is always horrid to me, but I don't care. I rise above her (that's what my Mum always tells me to do "Rise above them sweetie and don't let their stupidity affect you.") I just ignore her. So, yes people can be horrid. So can flowers I suppose. Once Stacy pushed me over on the playing field, right up in the far corner so no teachers would see, and I fell into lots of flowers and then my arms and legs went all red and spotty and started to get really big, and they hurt too. They were horrid flowers and my Mum told me that if I saw any other flowers that looked like those I should "Stay well away from them", she said I must be "Allergic" to them. I saw one horrid flower on telly that ate lovely little creatures. It had a big mouth with big teeth and it just swallowed little mice whole. That was horrid. But I have never seen a dead mouse on telly.

Maybe I should call the telly people up on the phone and get them to put my dead mouse on the telly. That would be cool. My dead mouse on telly, wait until Stacy found out! She would be so angry, she hates it when people do things, or have things better than her. Mum says it is because Stacy hasn't been "fortunate in what God has given her." I don't know what that means but I think it means that Stacy's house is smaller than ours, Mum calls Stacy's house a "Hovel".

My home is great. It's my Mum and Dad's house, but they say that I can call it my home forever. The only thing that isn't good in my home is when we have mashed potatoes for dinner, I hate mashed potatoes because they have no flavour and they are boring. But now, of course, there is the dead mouse as well, and that's not a good thing. It is kind of squidgy and yucky. It's got blood on it and it doesn't look very happy. I touched it! Not with my skin, that would be sick, I might catch something and it would definitely feel horrid. It looks horrid. I just poked it with my foot. I had my shiny black shoes on, not my best ones that have little flowers over my toes. These are my old best shoes. They are just plain shiny black.

I poked it and it rolled over. It was all floppy,

and on the side that had been on the floor it was all squidgy and covered with sticky blood. Well, not entirely covered. But there is a large patch of bright red blood on it. A little creature like that couldn't have much blood in it, or it would be all fat and wobbly and when it touched something sharp it would burst and make a real mess. So one mouse can't have much more blood in it than this one has on the outside of it.

I didn't like the way it looked up my skirt when I poked it with my foot. I was just rolling it over to get a better look at its face and it rolled its head over and looked right up my blue and yellow skirt. I panicked a little. I accidentally kicked it. I didn't mean to, it was just that when it looked up my skirt it scared me and I squealed and kicked out at it.

I don't want to touch it again, not even with my shoes on. When I moved it I couldn't feel it but I could tell it was all floppy, so I don't want to touch it again in case I can tell anything else.

It was a little bit outside my house. I had walked passed it not really seeing it properly. But then it caught the corner of my eye and I turned around and there it was. I had stepped back afraid, but when I crouched down to see it I had seen how sad it looked and that was when I went nearer to it and poked it. Then I got all scared and now I have kicked it inside my house. It flew through the air and thudded into the door inside my house and flopped down onto the floor. I feel bad about kicking it, but now it is in my house and I don't want yucky things in my house, not mashed potato and not a dead mouse.

After it landed it stopped looking at me. Now it is rolled up sitting on its head, as though it is half way through a gambol. It still doesn't look happy and I am sure that it can't be comfortable. It wasn't me that made it unhappy; it was sad and dead when I first saw it. But now I don't feel happy, because the mouse isn't happy and I haven't helped at all. I don't think that I could have made it happy, but I think I should have done better than kicking it.

I don't want to touch it again; it didn't help the

first time and it wont help a second time. There is a red smudge on the door where the mouse thudded before landing inside my house. A little red dot is on the ground outside my house where it had been before I kicked it. Inside there is carpet on the floor, I had better get Mum before that gets a red dot too.

It's tidied up now. Mum was funny, but a little bit bad too, I think. She screamed, but in a funny way, and then she pulled a funny face. That made me laugh. Then she got the dustpan and brush out of the kitchen and tried to brush the dead mouse onto the pan. But the brush was soft and just rolled the mouse onto the pan leaving a line of blood along the carpet. The brush hairs got some blood on them too. We both screamed a little at that, but then we giggled. Later I thought that was wrong, the giggling.

Nobody giggled at my Grandad's funeral when he died. And I wasn't allowed to play tig with the other children who were there either.

Mum got serious then, because she was cross about the mess, I said I was sorry but she smiled and said it wasn't my fault but Tibby's (Tibby is our cat) and anyway she had made it worse herself. Then she took the mouse and threw it in the dustbin outside. I had kicked it and now my Mum was throwing it in the bin. Our family hadn't treated the mouse very well at all. I think what my Mum did was worse than what I did.

Mum cleaned the door with a cloth and shampooed the carpet. I watch her shampoo the carpet. It was like shampooing the dog, except the dog wriggled and jumped about making more mess. The carpet lay still and let Mum do what she wanted. It didn't shake the water off at the end either and Mum had to try and dry the carpet. She whispered quietly about the cat while she dried the carpet, and she said swear words. I don't know why. She doesn't normally say swear words, well only sometimes, when she is really angry.

Now I am thinking about the mouse. It must be sad. When I heard Mum say swear words about the cat it made me sad, and I cried. Mum said she was sorry, but that it was the cat that had killed the mouse and so the mess was the cat's fault. Then she said she wouldn't hurt the cat because it was just doing what it wanted to do. I didn't really understand that because when I wanted to have a computer she had told me that we can't always have what we want.

Later she said that if I wanted we could take the mouse out of the bin and bury it in the garden in a margarine tub. It would be a proper funeral just like Grandad. I asked if we could have a gravestone but she said no. So I said it didn't matter. I just thought the mouse had been thrown around enough already, anyway, tomorrow the bin men come and they will take him away to the rubbish tip. I am sure that there are lots of mice at the tip and maybe he won't be so sad anymore.

3

Short and sweet that one. Don't get fooled, those first two are similar but from here on in they start to get different, bigger and better, and you'll start to understand why I'm doing this.

As I said earlier this next one was written while SD Downs lived in Szentes but is set in Kiskunhalas. I have found several versions of this story, including the hand written version in very messy handwriting alluded to in the introduction, but what I'm giving you appears to be the final completed product.

It presents itself as a true story that SD Downs has found and while I have discovered many of the locations and people referred to in it to be real I suspect, from the style of the telling and the eventual subject matter, that it is at most only semi-autobiographical.

I think he was just playing with the "discovered story" idea and it's actually his take on a gothic horror story or even an attempted parody of one. It had several different titles as it progressed, the final one presented here being "Wolf Hung". It's first title however was "How I became a Werewolf" and now I've given that away you'll see why I don't think it's a real story but just a story story.

That's one of the hardest things, looking back at what happened, trying to figure out if what you are looking at is part of the story of what happened or if it's just part of a story. Sometimes I think it can be both too. Having travelled around a bit I can tell you that the explanations about what happened vary wildly from place to place. I think it might depend on what "country" they come from.

Most sources agree about most of the physical things, and they add up with what's been left behind. But they often disagree about the order in which they happened, who did them and the reasons why they did them.

Every place agrees about the EMP
bombs. And the fact that hardly
anything works is the physical proof
that backs up the truth about them.
I'm not sure how the computer I am
working on survived, that must be
down to SD Downs along with the
power supply and everything else
that I have found here. For sure,
he must have sorted all this out
after the EMP's.

Every place agrees that EMP bombs
were used but all of them say that
they were attacked first and that
they sent theirs in retaliation.
I've read up on this extensively.
EMP means Electro Magnetic Pulse.
It's caused by a nuclear explosion
and it breaks everything that uses
electricity.

To begin with the big countries with
all the stuff built nuclear bombs
and put them in rockets to threaten
the other countries to help them get
stuff and to help them keep their
stuff. They even relied on
something called the "MAD strategy",
what they were doing was mad and
they knew it and called it MAD.

MAD means "Mutually Assured Destruction", basically they all had enough nuclear bombs in rockets that they could destroy any country that they wanted to and the only reason they didn't do it was because the other countries also had enough nuclear bombs in rockets to destroy their country. Totally insane.

Eventually someone realised exactly how insane it was and that the only thing using nuclear bombs could possibly do is totally destroy the entire world and as they didn't have any place else to live at that point it would mean they'd all be totally destroyed as well.

So, they fiddled with their rockets to make the nuclear bombs go off before they hit the ground so the explosion didn't destroy everything and everyone and leave the whole place unusable because it was covered in nuclear radiation. Instead the place was just hit by the EMP from the nuclear bomb which destroyed all the stuff that ran on electricity, and by this time EVERYTHING ran on electricity.

Anyway it was a bit of a dud idea.
Once one country did it all the
other countries did it too. And
then they just spent all their time
fixing electrical stuff until they
could do it again to get their own
back on whoever they thought had
done it to them. It maybe wasn't as
catastrophic as MAD but it was just
as mad as MAD.

And this was all going on at the
same time as the Climate Change
Catastrophe. I'm sorry, I'm getting
really off point again here aren't
I? My waffle must be completely
boresome for you. You know about
EMP bombs and the CCC, you're alive
here and now so of course you do.
What got me onto all that stuff?

Stories being stories or stories
being the real telling of something
that really happened and the way it
happened and the mixing up of all of
that. Because of "Wolf Hung", which
I'm pretty sure (and think you'll
agree) is mainly made up story with
a tiny bit of "real" thrown in to
help it be good. You read it now
and see what you think:

Wolf Hung

Word Count: 7588

By SD Downs

Szentes 2021

Intro

After I finished university my soon to be wife
convinced me to apply for a job with the British
Council as a TEFL worker abroad. We had
interviews on the same day in London and were both
accepted and sent to teach in schools in Hungary.
When we arrived we were given a crash course in
Hungarian and in how to teach language, this lasted
for one week and then we were picked up by
representatives from the schools we were to teach at
and taken out to the villages where we would live for
the year. Upon arrival in my village I was settled in a
small flat which I was told had been put aside by the
townsfolk for native foreign languages speakers, such
as myself, who had come to teach. I didn't find the
manuscript from which I have copied the following
text until my third or fourth week in residence. It was
stuffed under the mattress, at first I could not read the
handwriting but eventually I think I managed to
decipher correctly most of what was written.

It is my uncertainness about the deciphering of the
awful handwriting that has led me to leave in the
terrible writing style and the many grammatical
errors, so as not to change any of the possible
meanings or facts held within the document. As far

as I can research it in my current location, the main facts held within the text are true to life and did happen. I have a copy of the newspaper referred to in the text and have spoken to eye witnesses to some of the events. Here follows my copy of that text:

I am not one to gossip, or tell stories or even one who likes to draw attention to himself; but... I have reason (good reason) to believe that one of the citizens of my current hometown is of a particularly dark, dangerous and frankly down right evil persuasion. Please, do not get me wrong. I am in no way suggesting a parade through the streets, people shouting and screaming, burning torches held aloft, god forbid, no. Well... not until I collect enough sticks anyway.

This is an occasional evil, through the months it lurks dormant and slowly, in cycle with the moon, I watch it transform. What was once a smiling, joking, sometimes drunk and often sexually deprived man starts to change. Perhaps my suspicions were first aroused by the amount of curly black hair plugging up the shower. It was only then that I started to more closely examine those that I lived with. At the time I was working in Hungary as a teacher of English for the natives. Three of us lived together in a flat provided for us foreign language experts.

Craig was a pale skinned young man with dark curly hair. He was of average height, average weight. He was happy in a kind of average manner.

He laughed, he made jokes, he argued. There was nothing about him to make me suspect him. Except... maybe it was nothing, but Craig did seem to have an unnaturally powerful voice. It is not that he shouted everything exactly, although he often did shout, but somehow his voice always seemed to carry further and more clearly than everybody else's.

Jake came across as a quiet young man most of the time. The sort of young man it would be safe to leave your daughter with. He was maybe a little taller than average, perhaps a little skinnier than average, certainly quieter than average. He had short dark hair, which he cut himself. He was clean-shaven and quite innocent looking. And yet... maybe it was just my imagination. Most of the time he was quiet, maybe too quiet. You know how the next-door neighbours of serial killers always say that they were quiet and kept themselves to themselves, he was a little like that. Sometimes this wasn't true; occasionally a transformation would take place. Jake would still be reasonably quiet, but an almost evil grin would spread across not just his mouth, but also his eyes and then his whole face. Then he would joke, and play around. Mostly, no always, this would happen at night; sometimes while we were all drinking but occasionally when we were not as well.

Just so the reader can picture the three of us I shall now give a brief, and modest, account of myself. I am of above average height, lean and muscular, there is perhaps something of a heroic look about me. I am more handsome than most and of a much higher intellect than average. I have an excellent temperament, I am humorous and yet can be most serious when the need arises. I am extremely well educated and this shows itself in my everyday demeanour. Normally I am highly observant as well. I have been likened to Einstein mixed with a little of Sherlock Holmes, a dash of Robin Williams and a great big dollop of Harrison Fords looks. And still, little was I prepared for what was about to befall me.

Jake's room was suspiciously tidy and his door was often intriguingly closed. Sometimes he would disappear from the flat for hours on end, his only excuse that he had been out "walking". He never mentioned the fact that sometimes he would come back all muddy and wet, his clothes shredded and tattered. He claimed that he took photos on these walks, although I never saw any evidence of this. Later he dropped all pretence and did not even take his camera with him mumbling something about soldiers stealing it or something.

Craig was more open and yet in some ingenious way also managed to hide more from us with it. Take his room for example, the only time the door was shut his mysteriously powerful voice could always be heard speaking half of a telephone conversation. Normally his door was wide open; and yet his room was as impossible to enter as though it were behind the locked doors of a vault in the Bank of England. This was due to the massive amounts of dirty laundry and complete crap spread about the room in a cunning fashion. How he ever found a place to sit down I will never know.

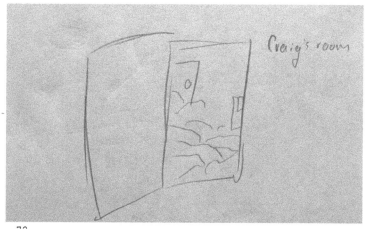

Craig's room

As well as walking and photography Jake had a keen interest in E-Mailing people and using the Internet, he also enjoyed reading. Craig too enjoyed reading, but both seemed to avoid any physical recreation of any sort. Myself, being an intelligent and somewhat heroic fellow, not only enjoyed the pleasures of reading and other art forms but also that of physical recreation. I thrive in all competitive sports and excel in anything I put my mind and brawn to.

We all enjoyed taking walks together, Jake would sometimes take his camera and Craig would take his wildlife book and astound us with his knowledge of plant and animal wildlife. I remember one particular occasion when we went on a walk together and saw a huge domesticated pig that had escaped the clutches of its owner (who was chasing after it down the road.) Craig wasted no time in coming to the well thought out conclusion of "JESUS! Look at the size of that HOG. ARRGH! It's coming this way. Shoo, you big fat pig, Shoo! Argh, run... run for your lives." So as you can see, he knew his stuff.

It was on that very same walk that Craig had taken samples of some curiously shaped leaves from some tall, thin plants. He told us that if you knew what you were doing you could use them in an almost medical manner. It sounded like he knew what he was talking about, and Jake too mentioned he had heard something similar about a similar looking plant.

So it was that we found ourselves meddling

with the science of nature that night, like a group of young kids (and a dog that talks) might meddle in a fake ghost mystery. I admit that I encouraged it; my profound sense of curiosity, my unnerving desire for adventure and my natural bravery all suppressing the deep dark foreboding that dwelt in the pit of my stomach like an angry duodenal ulcer ready to explode. I prepared the rolling papers as Craig selected the correct parts of the leaves with Jake's help. They cut and mixed them sufficiently before the final effort of rolling the joint of eternal wonderment, excitement and adventurousness. This was administered, and I must admit that now I look back I think that I must have felt nothing. At the time I believed that I had had a little new feeling in my head. I have no doubt now that this was the duodenal ulcer of my concern having crawled up my stomach and oesophagus to grab me by the brain and scream at me that what I was doing was wrong.

Whilst all of us described the sensations that we were experiencing I seem to remember a little alcohol was partaken to enhance the senses. Then a little more, and finally we retired to the Mini-Café, a near by bar which had become our local place of regular consumption of fermented vegetable drinks, to discuss what had happened to us over a couple of beers and a few whisky (or in my case vodka)

chasers; and a friendly game of cards (a Forint a point).

It was maybe two weeks later before any more of the story unfolded. I remember that I was in my study at the time diligently going over some notes for the next day's lessons when a terrible shriek sounded. It led me away from my work and into the corridor where I bumped into Jake. We glanced at each other and without a word, as one, we ran to Craig's room. Upon peering through the doorway (his floor being particularly unnavigable that day, some excuse about a parcel from home was the cover story for the food boxes and toilet paper that littered his floor) we perceived Craig standing at his empty sock draw; his socks were on the floor. He was holding a plastic bag in his right hand containing a white mouldering, moist, bubbly mess. He quickly explained that the bag had once contained his plant sample but somehow it had become active, through contamination of some sort he feared. He further hypothesised that our cleaning maid (Icá) may have sprayed polish on it.

Even though I doubted it (I had only ever seen Icá mopping the carpet, I doubt that she owned a dusting cloth let alone a spray can of polish) I joined Jake in consoling Craig. It was probably my charitable good nature and natural humbleness that encouraged me to do so. After some sobbing and grief induced illogical swearing and gnashing of teeth, not to mention a little Jim Beam, Craig came to the conclusion that he could wipe it off a bit and use it right there and then. We went through the preparations once more, the preparation of the rolling paper now familiar to me. There was a little added scrapping off of the wet bits and once more we were at the self-administration stage. I believe now that I felt even less than the nothing that I had originally felt upon my second active contact with the substance. But this time Craig professed greater sensations; "maybe the wet bits helped" was his comment. At the time I put Craig's enthusiasm down to the considerable amount of Jim Beam, mixed with a nasty measure of Black Velvet. But even Jake appeared, to me, to be acting a little stranger than normal.

Maybe I am wrong, and it was my powers of observation and perception that had changed; but I doubt it, I am very strong in this area. My mind is extremely clear and incredibly level. Once more we retired to the Mini-Café, to partake of some alcoholic beverages and pursue our activity of card playing (a Forint a point). Now, as I looked about me, it was not I or my colleagues who acted strangely but the proprietors of the Mini. The Mini is our regular haunt being not more than 10 metres from the front door of our flat. Being so positioned it enables a greater quantity of mental exercise (or "fun" as Craig would insist on calling it) to be had without having to sleep in the gutter. The girls who served us had become our good friends, despite the language barrier, and would often attempt to guess our orders in order to please us. On this night however a new lady was to attend to our table in the establishment. As we prepared to dual once more through the medium of cards (a Forint a point) an unearthly smell began to waft our way. It was an all too recognisable concentration of a sea salty, sweaty mixture. As the smell invaded our privacy the new girl attempted to give us her attention before throwing us out into the street for playing with cards (a Forint a point).

We moved on to a more distant and less hospitable place named "The Bar Behind The Spar". We were completely in wonderment at this treatment, and did not know what to think. We had become used to the inquisitive stares and were even able to accept a little abuse from our students when we saw them in the street, but this! It was completely different, being forced to flee the Mini; the Mini was sacrosanct. It was our home from home, it was our privacy. To have our privates exposed, chopped off and then taken away from us, in public, was the worst thing that we could imagine happening to us. Being thrown out of the Mini was a close second.

All that we saw seemed to have shifted its reality from the last time that we had looked at it, it was as though our eyes had changed, but they had not, and we knew so. As I look back I link this change not to a change in us but in the reaction from the people around us to something different in us. We sat stunned, large beers left on the table, its flavour soured, the cards dull, flat and lifeless in our hands, our pile of Forints lay cold in the centre of the table.

In short we retired quickly to our flat and slept. Few words were passed between us. We continued our lives. Rising early to teach, eating, studying hard to aid us in our teachings and sleeping. It was plain to all of us that something had changed.

We became more despondent with our jobs, Craig and Jake both, at times, questioned the reasons behind their coming here. For myself I would say that at this time I might have become negligent of my duties as an educationist. We took to drinking earlier and earlier. Craig started to smoke a pipe, in an urge to fulfil the herbal habit he could no longer act out as the plants had all died out in the first snow of the year earlier that week. We retreated further into our flat, venturing out less and less until all that we left the flat for were our jobs and food.

As I mentioned we started to neglect our educational duties. We were always there to teach, I never missed a class, but now we all prepared little, if at all, instead we spent the time gathered together in the study which had now become a church to all technological and space aged things. Together we had purchased the very best in audiovisual entertainment equipment. We could interact in games or simply watch and listen. It was all too easy to do apparently nothing. I do, however, recall some of what we watched and played and even now I can understand how at the time I believed it to be a good, healthy, intellectual pursuit. Few of you will have played with such technological advances, for they are not so common outside of the great technological state of Hungary, but no doubt most of you will have heard about the wonders that are Cartoon Network. This was just the beginning for us; there were late night old film channels and constant dodgy German televisual programming. This may give you an insight into the sort of intellectual stimulation that we had succumbed too.

A further two weeks passed in this way and we reached the Winter break. In our more active days we had all made ambitious plans for this period, and now we carried out these plans. We separated and set our minds to those actions thought of when our minds and bodies were much more animated. Jake travelled to Germany and Craig... well Craig travelled far and wide; I do not think that Jake or I really knew the extent of Craig's plans. Myself, I had a friend from home visiting me and I was to show him the wonders of Hungary. This time travelled slowly, like a snail going up a 90-degree slope covered in strawberry jam carrying heavy Gym equipment for his new fitness centre. How our shells did not break under the weight of that gym equipment I will never know. I can only guess that snail shells are made from a stronger compound than I had previously thought, perhaps some amalgamation of titanium and carbon, or the like.

Jake returned early. He may have mentioned that he would before he left but I do not remember. We spent a sombre, but not sober, New Year's eve in the company of my friend from England and some other Americans who were hanging about the place at the time. I did not really know who they were, and I am not sure that Jake did; I think that he just took pity upon them while they were visiting such a country and welcomed the opportunity to have a flavour of home. We felt little joy at the thought of a new year in this place, which had seemed to transform itself against us, and into something terrifying, and not a little scary.

Upon Craig's arrival from such far away places as I could not describe, and the departure of the last of our guests a warm blanket seemed to be drawn over the events of before and we attempted to forget our fears and confusion's. We attempted to start the New Year with a fresh mind, a clean slate; we wanted to live the life that we had begun back in the sunny September. The excessive gathering and compulsive partaking of the technological and audio visual systems remained, but Craig's pipe smoking habit was broken as for a couple of days he was violently ill. I think all in that building could hear just how violently ill he was, at least five times during his first night back and a further four times during his first morning. By then he was simply dry heaving, there was nothing left in his stomach, but his stomach itself, and he soon learned to quieten those noises, to give him his full credit.

Curiously the date of Craig's return coincided exactly with the fullness of the moon, as had been the case upon the day of the strange actions from our townsfolk (this I found out later as I have recently begun to study these events). I doubt many of you will know that the lunar month in question was an incredibly unusual and rare one. I have found out a little of this in the course of my research, but cannot profess to be an expert. Basically it was a peculiarly long lunar month in which the moon was the closest to earth that it has been since records began. It was something that had not been predicted and is still under analysis by the experts. During this time there was a much longer than normal gap between full moons, those who know a little about this thing will have heard of the "Periof" effect, although I myself can not understand its concept fully. It is enough to state that it was an unusually long time during which we were under stronger than normal effects from the moon.

Craig's illness disappeared as suddenly as it had appeared. It was as if his body needed to adapt itself once more to life in our town as though there were an airborne disease present only in that village, if you lived with it constantly you became immune; but if you had little contact with it... well, it made you throw up really violently. His body soon remembered these foreign invaders to his body and adapted to cope with them once more.

Soon after his recovery there was a day of

celebration. I forget now what the cause of this may have been; perhaps it was somebody's birthday or some sort of National holiday in Hungary. Whatever, we celebrated to the max. We started in our flat, imbibing a few fermented vegetable drinks, by the time we hit the Mini we were well into our stride. Not being a weak-minded fool I know my limits, vast as they are, when it comes to alcohol and am strong minded enough to resist addiction of any sort. While I cannot speak so strongly for my colleagues, I can vouch that until that time they had shown themselves to be my equal in at least this matter. But on this night we were all to lose control in some way.

We all rose well after midday on the Saturday (the celebrations having taken place on the Friday night). I have always been able to cope with extremes and excesses without serious effects upon my physical well-being. I awoke energetic and clear headed to the sounds of Jake vomiting. Violently. Apparently Craig had perfected the art of quiet self-purging, for though the shower room was silent and the door locked, an odour of vomit transpired from under the door. Later their conditions would be diagnosed as "seriously Hung Over". Until then I had to listen to the complaints about the noise of Jake dry heaving from the people on the top floor (we live on the ground floor, incidentally it was the first time the people from the top floor had spoken to me). Indeed even the bath specialist prostitute who lived in the flat above ours came down to see what was going on. She said that we had been "enhancing" her work, and she enquired if I would like to join her in looking for "a good time". This did not make sense, maybe I mistranslated it; how, and why, would I try to look for a good time? Time is not an object and cannot be pin pointed in any physical form.

As we congregated for the first solid food of the day (a hamburger from "Hun Burger", the most stomach settling food that had come to my mind) at around six in the evening, we tried to discus the events of the previous evening. We all remember up to the point when we left the Mini at closing time and decided to travel to the 24-hour place on the main street. It had very cheap drinks and electronic Black Jack, which Craig always triumphed upon. Craig had found his wallet and managed to prove that we had made it as far as the 24-hour place as he had a few thousand more Forints than he had started the evening with. So once more Craig had triumphed over the machine, and then... Well even between us we could not account for what had happened or how we had arrived back home. It was then that I revealed that I could not find my clothes. A quick search revealed them to be nowhere within our flat. I had hoped, at worst, to find them vomit stained and smelly in some corner, nook or cranny. To not find them at all was perplexing. "Have you got your wallet?" they asked me. I had found it on the floor of my bedroom, with what looked like teeth marks in it, I communicated this to them. "Weird!" Craig commented holding up his own wallet which he still had hold of after looking to see how much money he had won from the electronic black Jack. His wallet had teeth marks as well

I remember distinctly the sly smiles and

comments, our self-satisfied grins, "we could have

done anything!" Only Jake showed any sign of negative emotions, fear or regret. "Doesn't that scare you in the least? You could have done anything and you don't even remember it."

"I know," replied Craig with a huge grin "I think it's great!"

"Even if you didn't do anything bad, even, and lets take the best case scenario here; even if you did nothing embarrassing but did great magnificent things, female conquests or whatever your fantasies are. Even then I don't see how you can grin so much. Surely you should be devastated, you could have slept with the best looking woman in the world, but you have no recollection whatsoever. The best moment of your life could have been lost forever. You don't remember a sweet moment of it." That seemed to sober Craig a little " And I am sure that we all agree that the best case scenario is really, really, really unlikely; more likely you did something terrible." Jake concluded. Looking back it seems a portent of things to come. My normally perceptive and level mind must have been under incredible pressure, as the best it could come up with was the joke "Of course she would have to have been one of your students." "Now that would be just my luck!" answered Jake. For some reason not only all the women, but also all the students seemed to fancy Jake as soon as they met him. "You see" began Craig in psychologist mode "you're just sad because of the repression of your sexual desires for your students, and now you think that maybe you lost control last night and you may have to deal with real life issues."

I remember those lines of dialogue as though

they had been burned into my brain with a laser, and everyday they have been replayed with no loss of quality, like a fully light oriented sound recording system which would require no touching parts and so the normal wear and tear of physical objects would not occur. The seriousness passed with our first jokes of the day. We continued joking through the Sunday, and Jake joked with us, until the next day. Monday. Midday.

I arrived back at the flat from work; the sun had been shining, though a good two centimetres of ice still covered the paths. My body was warm and sweaty under my coat, gloves and scarf from walking quickly. My thighs were burning from the lactic acid and my cheeks were numb from the cold wind. Jake was already in the flat, calmly drinking a glass of milk and reading in the kitchen. In the staff room I had found the front cover of the newspaper "Népszabadság" covered with the headline "THIRTEEN TORN TO DEATH". Below is a rough translation that I wrote at the time, my Hungarian at that time was far inferior to what it is presently but unfortunately I did not keep the original:

"   13 citizens of Kiskunhalas were found torn to pieces together in a field on the East edge of the town last night. An initial examination of the bodies at the Kiskunhalas hospital revealed that while the bodies had certainly been further mutilated by wild animals of some sort the actual cause of death was not yet certain. Dr Joszeph Bánfi of the hospital announced in the early hours of the morning that while initial reports had indicated an animal related incident there were some injuries that did not conform to this theory and the possibility of another source of

death had yet to be ruled out. He
continued that the marks that had
obviously been made by an animal
seemed to be from a very large
carnivore, and that he did not know
of any creatures large enough living
in this area. Suspicion has been
heightened by the report of a group
of seven missing teenagers last
being seen involved in an argument
with some young men "Not from these
parts"."

There was more, but as I have stated I did not keep

the original and my language skill had yet to mature

fully.

I showed the paper to Jake, who continued

sitting calmly, occasionally drinking milk from his

glass as I flapped about the kitchen. "What's your

problem? Do you think we did that?" He looked at

me with disbelief in his eyes. So the thought had

crossed his mind as it had screamed through mine

when I had first seen the paper. And yet he was so damnably calm "They died in the early hours of Saturday. Just those hours that we can not recall." I snapped, "Even though I realise that I" I emphasised the "I" before continuing "I am not capable of this, they were at the 24 hour place, where we were. We have no alibi and if we saw anything we don't remember it." I was quite out of my mind with panic at that point. He shrugged and I seethed. He finished his drink and refused to comment further on the matter retreating to his room and shutting the door.

I sat in the kitchen and calmed down a little. Even with my considerable knowledge of martial arts could it have been possible for the three of us to have done this, I was not as convinced of my innocence as I had communicated to Jake. When I was younger I was known amongst my peers as having a dreadfully strong temper that was quick to rise, they had nicknamed me "Freak out Freddy". As I have grown I have managed to tame, at the very least, the manner in which my temper manifests itself, and whilst I still have a dreadful temper it takes me a huge amount of time and pressure to become anywhere near angry. As I reasoned it out, I saw that our greater worry was that we may have been witnesses to something and we could not even account for our whereabouts at that time. Where were my clothes? The thought struck me like a blow; my heart seemed to stagger under the blow. What if they were amongst the bodies? What if they were somewhere near the bodies? I banged on Jake's door.

He allowed me to enter after seeing that I had

calmed down a little and listened as I explained my thoughts to him, ending with the unknown location of my clothes. As I said this last a "manic Jake" grin spread across his face, gleaming in his eyes "I don't have my clothes from that night either!" It was the first time he had admitted this. So I was not the only one. I quickly and intently questioned him as to their location "Don't worry about it, I have a fairly good idea where they are." his grin beamed at me. He bade me leave his room again and instructed me to disturb him again only once Craig had returned from his place of work. I could not help but notice as I left the room that Jake had been studying some of Craig's nature monographs as they were spread across his desk with book marks sticking out from between the pages. He reopened the one that he had held in his hands while I had been with him and waved me out of the room

      Craig returned home an hour earlier than was normal for him on a Monday. He found me in the kitchen, he was in a highly agitated mood as he too clutched a copy of the newspaper, which I had seen, and expressed his worries in a much less coherent form than I had managed. I was able to understand that one of the students from his final Monday class was amongst the missing teenagers, who had now been identified as seven of the dead people. I managed to sedate him a little before knocking on Jake's door. Jake came into the kitchen with messy hair, I had awoken him, and a very self-satisfied look upon his face. With a smug commanding voice he told us to put on our coats and to follow him on a little walk. Craig and I exchanged looks but said nothing as we collected together our hats and coats.

We lived just outside the very centre of Kiskunhalas; our flat was a four-minute walk to the cinema, which was the central grand edifice of the town. We followed Jake directly East through the centre of the town and out to the outer regions passing one of Craig's schools on the way. We turned left when we reached the main bypass road. Along this road lay some of the more exclusive pubs and clubs of the town. We followed the road passing the Goose Guarded House then the Fishy Bar, which looked like a brothel but was just a bar really. If we had turned right we would have arrived at the 24-hour place, but we just continued on our leftward journey. Further on and we passed the "Slap Slap Girlies" club which looked like a strip club to me, maybe because of the 9 foot neon letters pronouncing "Non-Stop Strip Club" under which a smaller notice contained the opening times: 22:00 - 06:00. It was in fact a brothel, not a strip club at all. All this time we walked in silence. As we passed the brothel Jake smiled to himself, and Craig stared hungrily at the door. Next we passed the circus, which had settled here for the past two weeks, a small affair with a handful of animals and a troop of clowns, jugglers and bad magicians. Craig and I had been to see a performance and I had thought it all rather pathetic and believed it be for little children only. Craig had been delighted, though, by the two bears that had performed minimal tricks before being given a bottle of beer each to drink. This last had Craig standing and cheering. He had looked like a six-year-old child who had been offered the keys to the toyshop and told to just take anything that he wanted. "Look at the bear" he had squealed, "It's drinking beer! It's a bear drinking beer from a bottle!"

Still we walked onwards, past the "Green House" lunatic asylum; lovingly referred to by our students as a "special place for all those socially disadvantaged and mentally underprivileged fellow human beings." We walked right out to the Halosító (fishy lake). "Ah! Breath in that fresh air boys." Jake filled his lungs after his first words since leaving the house. "Now, somewhere here lies the solutions to all of our questions." He walked us clockwise around the lake until we had walked out onto a small peninsula type place that almost split the lake into two separate lakes. The ground was frozen mud; the air stank and was filled, even at this time of the year, with nasty evil biting insects. Growing thickly all around the edge of the lake were tall grasses the names of which I did not know.

When we were almost at the water Jake smiled, pointed and then shouted "THERE THEY ARE BOYS! ALL YOUR ANSWERS." Craig ran and almost fell over in a small clearing on the waters edge where our frozen clothes lay scattered about the place, muddy, and in some cases torn a little. Our clothes mingled together in no order on the floor of this clearing surrounded by the tall grasses. We had been walking on a path broken through these grasses, I noticed now, and I could see that the ice had been broken and then had frozen again at the waters edge. Had we really gone into that icy cold water? "Now, for what it's worth, here is my guess" started Jake "I have some small recollections now that have helped. We arrived at the 24-hour place, as planned, and once more Craig triumphed on the electronic Black Jack game. In his drunken state he decided that after winning once more he must run screaming from the place in a subtle bid to avoid losing the money"

"Yeah, that's right," Craig started slowly, "I remember that bit now. I was so drunk that I thought, for some reason, that if I stayed they would take the money off me."

"Excellent. Now, Simon and I followed you, caught up with you and then together we headed towards the biggest magnet for all drunkards: The Strip Club!"

"Except it's not, it's a brothel." I added helpfully.

"Yes! Exactly. We left, pissed off and still very drunk, and wandered out here, in the wrong direction for home, and when we saw the lake decided a swim would be good. Then, here is the worst news, rather than tearing a bunch of people apart we decided a spot of nude running would be the best way to get home and it would sober us up." Jake looked at us triumphantly. Craig's eyes brightened and then dimmed as he started slowly "I have this remembrance.   I remember thinking I mustn't get my money wet. I remember putting my wallet in my mouth, biting on it and thinking to myself that I mustn't bite too hard as I could break my plastic cards." Craig spoke from far away, wonder and amazement at his own recollections evident in his voice. "That's it. I don't remember anything else. I don't remember swimming or..." his voice trailed off and then he continued, "I remember running. I remember running so hard that my bare feet hurt and my lungs felt like they would burst, except that they were so numb that it didn't matter." Jake stepped

forward "And Simon and I followed you."

"JESUS! JESUS CHRIST!" Craig's exclamation was

swallowed by the cold dank air hanging over the lake

"I hadn't even realised that my clothes were missing,

JESUS!" He howled like a wolf "OOOHHHH

MMAN! We were drunk OUT OF CONTROL! But

we didn't kill anybody!" His relief was obvious, as though he had really thought it the most plausible explanation, that he had murdered 13 people. My relief was not so swift; I still could not remember a thing.

Jake turned to me "That is our story Simon. That's our alibi. There's no way we were involved, we were too drunk, too stupid, and too wet and nude. Dumb and embarrassed, but not murderers, not killers." Jake nudged me and winked. I was stunned "But how did you figure all this out? How much can you remember? Everything?" I questioned.
"No, still hardly anything, but I heard a little punk kid at my primary school telling all his rock stupid friends a story that had them in fits of laughter all lesson. At the end I kept him back and had him tell me all about

it. He lives in that house over there" Jake pointed to a wooden two story building at one end of the lake "he looked out of his window in the night and saw us running around butt naked. He told me that, then I told him to go, the other kids hadn't believed him anyway. Then I had this vague memory of an argument we tried to have with one of the girls in the strip club"

"The brothel" I corrected helpfully.

"You were trying to get her to strip by offering her Craig's money and he had run just like he had in the 24 hour place. Even though I was drunk I can remember thinking that it was lucky cause she was butt ugly anyway. And that's it."

When Jake finished speaking he spread his hands out in front of him and in the moments of silence that followed as he stood like that we all began to laugh. We laughed loud and we all relaxed. I was really relieved and the others were too it seemed; the relief let itself out with laughter. We packed the stiff, frozen clothes in plastic bags that Jake magically produced from his pockets and walked home joking and laughing. When we got home the laughter continued. It wasn't a hysterical laughter, but a calm, relaxed, happy laughter that continued around us as we put the clothes in the washing machine. Then Jake showed us the teeth marks in his wallet and this brought on more fits of laughter. We forgot all about the change that had happened in the town and from that time onwards the rest of our stay was as it had been when we had first arrived. Except that instead of three strangers living together we were now all old friends who had known each other forever and were now living together; always joking and laughing.

We never talked to each other about the killings again, even though it was a big story in that little town. Hell, it was a big story in that little country. I watched the papers in the staff room as more information was released. Seven girls, six boys, eight of them from local schools the others from smaller close by villages. A scandal scattered the evidence from the case; a large amount of alcohol had been found in the blood from some of the bodies, a large enough amount to have killed a person. This was traced to a mess up by one of the doctors and most of the evidence that they had found was deemed unusable. The doctor was fired... from that department but continued working in the hospital as a gynaecologist rather than whatever it was he had been before.

In the end the story the police put together was of death by stupidity, or misadventure or whatever. A drunken argument, they decided, had occurred outside the 24-hour place and then two groups had gone off to a field to fight it out without the interference of the police. During the fight or after the fight the groups had been attacked by some passing wild animals, or maybe one or both groups collected dogs on their way and this accounted for the eventual deaths and horrible mess. Staff room gossip pointed the finger at the circus and the bears but nothing was ever said officially on this, although there was a note about wanting to speak to the circus people who had left town by then. I don't know if they ever contacted them. After all that, the story left the front page and the gossip channels in my school. I never felt any guilt.

At the end of the year I was head hunted by another school in a nearby town and I accepted the wage and responsibility increase. Craig went off travelling once more and Jake went home to America, Madison, Wisconsin. I still keep in touch, occasionally. Craig passed through Hungary again a couple of weeks ago and I met him. Something in his manner was different. It was the same old Craig; but deep down... I could see it deep in his eyes when they met mine for too long. Out of nowhere, a long silence, he confessed that he had faked his memories of that night. He said that he just wanted what Jake was saying to be true, and he thought that he might prompt us to remember by remembering something himself. But he hadn't recollected everything that he had said. He had vague memories of running with the wind rushing through his hair and feeling free, but that was it. He said that he had seen the teeth marks on his wallet in the morning and couldn't find his clothes and was plain scared shitless. He had stayed that way, the newspaper only reinforcing the terror within him, until Jake had taken us to our clothes. He said that he had started sleeping badly as soon as he had left our company, that when he tried to sleep a deep down guilt in his gut just nagged him. It wasn't pain, he explained, but it was like Chinese water torture and he was scared that eventually it would get to him. "Sometimes it seems to go away, but then a couple of weeks pass and it just starts to build up again." I remember him saying with a deep pained look upon his face.

I sat stunned, and yet not surprised, my thoughts had often gone back to it. Then he said something that did surprise me. He said that HE thought HE had done something terrible. Not me, or us but HIM! That shocked me.

After he left I started to have a little trouble sleeping as well. I had never had any memories from that night, and now I found that neither had Craig, apart from a vague memory of running and feeling free. That left Jake. How much did he remember? Not a lot, he had confessed so himself, and how much of what he did remember did I believe? How much did I believe Jake? An inner voice started nagging me whenever things around me became quiet.

Yesterday the moon was full and close once more, some left over effects from last year. This morning on the TV I heard on CNN: *"5 Die in what police are calling an animal attack of some sort. The police in Madison, Wisconsin have put out a warning to be on the look out for a large wild animal, possibly a bear or a large cat, which may have escaped from a local zoo. Representatives from the zoo have been quiet but have made a small statement announcing that as far as they know none of their animals are missing."* I bought Népszabadság (Hungarian national newspaper) on my way to work and found the headline: `"7 DEAD IN SMALL TOWN SZENTES"` on the cover, Szentes is the new town I find myself in now. The article started with the the words: `"7 bodies were found torn apart by wild animals early in the..."`

Craig was heading for Africa when he left me. I have been trying to find out if any such attacks have been reported there, but animal attacks are a bit more common there and there are lots of out of the way places where nothing ever gets reported. But I am certain, so certain, that if I look hard enough I will find some sort of corresponding maniacal occurrence. I lost hours this evening, without noticing the passing of time, while I stared in turn first at the teeth marks in my new wallet and then at the empty laundry basket in the corner of my room that should contain my soiled clothes from last night. I fear to sleep tonight, for truly do I know that one of the citizens of my current home town is of a particularly dark, dangerous and frankly down right evil persuasion. And I fear him, I fear him and what actions he has performed in the past. If it wasn't for the other two I could happily kill myself to save the people I know I may harm in the future, but I know that first I must find and stop the other two. This is the only action that can focus and calm my mind now. I must go.

4

What did you think? That was a
longer more story driven story, I
mean the first two were sketches
where as this was more of a studied,
detailed drawing. Eventually he
begins to fill massive canvases with
multicoloured, multilayered, bright
colours and subtle undertones. But
at this point you can still tell
that he is just playing with story
writing; trying out different styles
and ideas; just having a bit of fun.

It was quite a long one that, I hope
you were ready for it. I'm trying
to build you up to the more complex
works. The next one is a short one
again, to give you a rest, and
another attempt at a different genre
style. Although, again, he doesn't
fully commit and tries to make a
joke out of it.

But it marks an important point in
SD Downs's life, he was living in
Budapest by the time he wrote it.
His girlfriend had become his wife

and he was working in a library,
like he had studied at university
for, rather than teaching. In the
few bits of journal that I have
found he mentions his year in
Budapest as being one of the best of
his life.

I have visited the library that he
worked at, it was in a building
belonging to a company called "The
British Council". "British" refers
to the country that was called
"Britain" which, as far as I can
tell, was itself made up of a group
of smaller countries grouped
together on an island. There isn't
much of it around anymore.

Britain had been really good at
collecting all the stuff from all
over the world and for a long time
it was one of the countries with the
most stuff. But then it started
losing its stuff and by the time of
the EMP bombs it was one of the
smaller countries.

At the time SD Downs was working at
the British Council library in
Budapest (still in Hungary)
"Britain" was still under the

delusion that it was a big country
with lots of stuff and so they sent
the British Council out to other
countries to teach them all how to
become "British" by speaking English
and reading their books.

I had a good scavenge at the library
but there wasn't much useful left.
The building had mostly been
converted into bomb shelter and most
of the bookcases were empty and had
been used to block up the entrances
and windows. There were a few in
the basement that still had some
books on.

As you'll all know physical, made
from paper, real books made a come
back (big time) after all the
events. Before the EMP bombs most
reading was done on electrical
devices but once they were all
broken people went back to paper.
But paper is terribly vulnerable to
water; it totally destroys books,
even just a little bit, over time.
Which is why the "Earth Friendly"
nuclear war was such a disaster for
reading and books.

I know you all know this, but it's

in my head now and I need to get it
out. The "Earth Friendly" nuclear
war was what happened when the only
countries that were left got bored
of throwing EMP bombs at each other.
Some bright spark decided instead of
detonating their nuclear bomb high
above a country they didn't like,
they could do it next to the country
but under water. Nuclear explosions
under the sea didn't leave the land
all covered in radiation, but it did
cause big tidal waves that poured
over the land killing people and
ruining all of the country that was
anywhere near the sea.

And this was after most of the
smaller islands and sea side
countries had already been lost
under the sea because of the big
CCC, Climate Change Crisis. The
world warming up and getting more
stormy had raised the sea level
sinking the edges of the land under
the water. Flooding the libraries,
destroying the books. Meaning far
fewer books and all the electronics
used to make new books broken and no
way to print new copies or make new
ones. And not many people left to
write new ones anyway.

Which was why I was so delighted to find any at all in the library at the British Council in Budapest. It was a good place to look for them. Hungary didn't have any coast even after the CCC and the only water damage happening in the Budapest library was from the weather which the basement bomb shelter was pretty well protected from.

Right, this next story. A short one, written for a competition. SD Downs had already won a short story competition at University and this story shows he was still entering them at the time he was living in Budapest. And that he was still trying out lots of different writing styles and genres. It's small but kind of fun.

30 in a Room

(A short Sam Shovel Detective Story)
Word Count: 1030

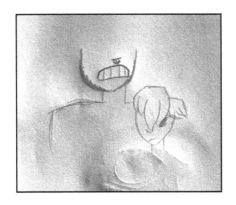

By SD Downs
Budapest 2022

Intro

Blending noir with the surreal, Sam Shovel is a literary creation that is obviously going nowhere and fast. Read all you'll ever need to know about him in this detective novel of one thousand and thirty words...   This is my entry in The Unofficial Short Story Competition

It was the Dame. It's always the Dame. The tall leggy blonde who saunters into my office and pouts her lips in that way I can't resist. I know they are nothing but bad news the moment I hear their stiletto heels on the stairs up to my office; but I just sit there and let them in anyway. My name's Shovel, and anyone who comes up with a gardening joke can go to hell, I've heard them all before and more besides. Maybe it was my name that lead me to become a Private Investigator, maybe it was my unnerving nose for trouble, one way or the other it doesn't matter, it's what I am and it's what I do.

She was everything that I would want in a woman, and everything that I'd tell my son to avoid, if I ever got close enough to woman again in my life to have a son. She gave me the same old sob story I'd heard a thousand times in my line of work and not a word of it was true, I could tell right from the first words she uttered. After she'd finished and wiped the last crocodile tears from her stunning blue eyes I accepted

the case and she just smiled her hollow smile at me. She paid cash and I asked no questions.

That was more than two weeks ago, and the tale of how that meeting led me to be imprisoned in a room with what I count as roughly 30 pigmy cannibals, all wanting me as the starter for a bloody meal of P.I. is a hell of a story but not one I have time for right now.

I'd scared the crowd away with the magic of fire from my trusty Zippo lighter, but I could see the braver few of the group edging forwards already and the Zippo was getting hot enough in my sweaty hand that I could smell my fingers starting to cook.

Damn it! I was doing their job for them, and as soon as my hand was done medium rare the lighter fuel would run out and I'd be stood in the corner of a dark room with nothing to protect myself but a crudely made explosive and nothing with which to light it but sheer will power and hope. I reached into my trench coat and pulled out the explosive. Their eyes turned as one and I thought I heard the air in the room thin as they all breathed in at the same time.

My home made gelignite had been lovingly crafted into a statuette of a naked Lara Croft by a game nerd I knew by the name of Mario O' Death. It wasn't his real name but some sort of code name he used in his secret online gaming clubs. He was the sort of person you wouldn't trust with your donut after he'd eaten all the donuts a human could possibly consume, but in a pinch he always had the skills to help you out. He'd found my secret explosives stash while I was out of the office when he had come over to borrow a sweat band he knew I had. He'd been playing a dance video game and his profuse perspiration had greased his dance mat until it was like an ice rink. Knowing nothing better he had assumed it was play dough and had got to work with the only inspiration he ever had in his mind, unrealistic personifications of the female form as portrayed through the medium of video game entertainment.

As the crowd stood transfixed by Lara's nudity I could have thanked the Lord, if that was my thing, but it isn't. Instead I just lit the fuse and threw the bomb to the nearest salivating pigmy cannibal. I turned intending to kick down the door and make good my escape but before I could the door swung open on its own and the Amazonian Dame who had got me here in the first place stood framed as the fizzing fuse of my bomb lit her like a cameraman's dream.

"I see you've met my orphan children" she said.

"What?" I replied.

"The kids." she said "These are the orphans I wanted your help with."

I gulped "You mean you were serious? You were telling the truth?" She raised an eyebrow and made a look like she was appraising my mind, body and spirit all in one. If I'd been the litigious type I'd have filed for sexual harassment there and then. "I thought it had all been a ruse... A cunning plan to get me in here, trapped with no escape, so you could get me out of the way and fulfil whatever evil plot it is you are trying to conclude!" My words bounced off of her like she were a battle ship and my words were the waves of the ocean.

She laughed, and I flinched as the bomb exploded with an almighty wet farting sound. I don't know exactly what happened next, I may never know. Maybe it was the shock of it all, maybe it was something in the fumes from my home made explosive, or maybe it was the fist of the dame dislodging something in my brain as she slammed it full force right on my nose. When I woke there were police. Lots of police. They'd drawn a chalk outline around me and the crime scene photographer was flashing as he took pictures of me. I fluttered my eyelashes and tried to make a Marilyn Monroe smile.

It didn't work. I was cuffed, booked, charged, convicted and cooling my heels in a cell before I had a chance to mumble 'Stop! Police brutality!'

At least I'd gotten out of that room with the 30 most evil looking creatures I'd ever seen. Of course now I had to survive the communal shower of the clink. One entrance, no exit, thirty shower heads pissing freezing cold water on me and 30 burly, hairy, tattooed criminal types blocking my escape all with the same thought on their mind. Hurt the child killer. Hurt me.

5

That one is quite silly really, just a bit of fun. Which actually links it quite well to the next one, which is very silly and, again, very short.

After Budapest SD Downs and his wife moved to London, the capital city of Britain, which was still above the level of the sea at that time. SD Downs worked in another library this time at a drama school and his wife had a baby, a son, the first of their three children together. I have pictures of them in their house in London with the new born baby, the most recent pictures in the "old PC stuff" file.

They all look really happy except in one picture where the baby is pulling a really unhappy face and SD Downs is laughing. It's a slightly odd photo that one.

He must have been very busy because there isn't very much writing from

this time, in fact this might be the
only complete story there is. He
didn't just work in the library he
was the manager of it. From his CV
(a list of all his jobs and
qualifications) that I found on the
Mac it sounds like he was their
first librarian and he built the
library for them. Pretty impressive
stuff.

At first I didn't think there were
any stories from this time but I
came across this one in his email
files. Years after he had written
it at the drama school he sent the
story in an email to another writer
who had written an article in a
magazine for librarians:

Reply

Subject: Stories from Librarians
Fri 22/08/2031, 10:49
xxxxx@xxxxxxxxxxx

Dear Sir,

My name is SD Downs, I've been a librarian
since 2020 when I graduated from
Loughborough University. I've bounced around

a bit (Budapest, London, Oxford and currently Wolverhampton) but have always ended up in a library of some sort in an educational institution. I saw the article in the CILIP gazette asking for stories from librarians and thought you might like the one below that I wrote whilst working at a drama school in London in 2023.

I'd been having problems getting a broken chair taken away by the caretaker. I put the broken chair outside the door of the library several evenings in a row but would come back the next morning to find it had been put back into the library so I wrote this story, stuck it to the chair and put it out once more. The chair got taken away within an hour.

It is called: The Sad Tale of Larry the Unhappy Chair *(Or: "The tale of the chair sitting outside of the library")*

It must have been amazing to be able to send messages all over the world electronically like that. They would get there almost instantly, including text, pictures, videos, pretty much anything.

Obviously once the EMP bombs started up all that stopped. Even though they could fix the electronic devices that sent them, or build new ones, the way they got sent around the world was by satellites,big electronic devices in space. And it was a lot harder to repair or replace them when they got broken by the EMP's. So electronic communication stopped.

It was back to paper. That seems to have been the big trend as the electronic world got more and more broken, paper became king and was used for everything. Just another contributing factor to why they chopped down all the trees so quickly (they made paper from trees) even though they are the lungs of the Earth and chopping them all down helped make the air go bad, the storms get worse and the sea rise and flood the land.

You might think some of these little stories by SD Downs are ludicrous and absurd but it's nothing compared to how humans were acting all those years ago. Looking around at everything in their world getting broken and starting to go bad and just carrying on doing all the things that are causing it.

It's like they were hanging off a cliff by one hand, and in their other hand they had an axe and instead of using it to help climb back up they were using it to chop off the hand holding them up thinking "ooh look, a hand, that could come in useful, I'd better get that". Seriously how could they not see what they were doing? And how much it was hurting themselves?

So, this story isn't quite that stupid but it is absurd. I see it as an absurdist attempt at a mini comic parable.

The Sad Tale of Larry the Unhappy Chair

(Or: "The tale of the chair sitting outside of the library")

Word Count: 1135

By SD Downs

ALRA 2023

Once upon a time there was an unhappy chair called Larry. Larry was unhappy because all he brought to the world was pain, misery, frustration, bewilderment and anger, not the nicest collection of emotions I am sure you will agree. Larry was a chair, but a chair that could never be used, for as you would be able to see from looking at him, he was broken. Now there isn't much use for a broken chair in a library, which was a bit of a shame as a library was where Larry lived. You see the problem with having a broken chair in a library is that people only see a chair and they try to sit on it, it is normally at around about this point that they discover it is not a chair, but a broken chair. It is also at around about this point that the pain, bewilderment and then slowly (sometimes not so slowly) anger start to present themselves.

As I am sure you can imagine, if you watched all of your peers succeed and excel in their chosen profession while you idly sit by and fail miserably, you would become pretty frustrated, and this is indeed where the frustration comes into this tale of woe and misery. It was this frustration over the pain, bewilderment and anger that caused the chair to be so miserable. So miserable that Larry was contemplating suicide.

One day Larry awoke and found himself once more in a prime location for his job, he was right in front of the main computer in the library, just awaiting a library user to sit upon him so that they could access the wondrous internet highway and discover all that their heart desired. But it was not a library user who first approached him with the desire of sitting in him this not particularly sunny morning; it was Simon the Happy Librarian. Larry loved Simon, for Simon was indeed as happy as he was a librarian and was never nasty to any of the chairs even the ugly or dirty chairs that didn't really fit in with the rest of the furniture.

Simon was the protector of the chairs of the library and he always did the best he could to save the chairs when they were stolen by the evil stage management students or by the nasty men who took them away to use them as torture devices in the dreaded "interviews". Just the thought of these evil people and evil actions brought shivers to the bravest of the plastic and synthetic leather folding chairs, and a rust inducing tear to the chrome metal and almost real leather chairs that dominated the main library space. All could remember the two friendly metal and wooden chairs who had recently disappeared without trace. Not even Simon seemed able to save them.

So you can imagine how happy Larry was to see Simon approaching him as his first seating buddy of the day. Then Larry remembered that he was broken and that if Simon were to try and sit on him he would be first in pain, then bewildered, then angry. Larry tried to shout out not to sit on him as he was broken, but as you may have noticed there are very few chairs that can actually speak and Larry was not one of these special speaking chairs. Simon came closer, and Larry began to panic, he couldn't warn Simon so maybe he could jump out of the way. Alas, try as he might, Larry could not move himself one inch, because as you may have observed in the world around you there are even fewer independently moving chairs than there are speaking chairs.

Simon sat. Simon felt the back give way. Simon felt the odd shaped bit of metal stick into his bottom and the sharp plastic shard prod his lower back. Simon felt pain. Simon felt bewildered. Then he started to feel angry.

"Oh bother", he said most angrily.

"It is that silly broken chair!" If it had been possible for a chrome and almost real leather chair to blush, Larry would have done so now, fancy being called "Silly" Larry had never seen Simon so angry or use such language before about the chairs.

"Why", said Simon "this silly broken chair does bewilder me greatly, every day I find it and I try to put it out of the way so nobody will get hurt by it and every day once more I find it in a place where somebody is bound to sit in it" Simon was fuming mad.

"It is almost as though those rascal students are putting you in these positions trying to hurt people" Simon smiled and then he laughed.

"No, those lovely studenty people would never do such a nasty thing, those studenty people are lovely. So how does this keep happening?" Simon wondered. Then, as often happened with Simon, he had a great idea.

"I've just had a great idea", said Simon

"I shall write a note for Mick the Nice Caretaker Man who is into Northern Soul Music" said Simon, for that was Mick's official title.

"Now then" said Simon "what shall I write?"

If it had been possible for Larry to tremble, tremble he would have done. What was to happen to him?

Mick the Nice Caretaker Man who is into Northern Soul Music was indeed a nice man, and was indeed also into Northern Soul Music, which by itself is no bad thing. But Larry had on more than one occasion seen him with hammers, electric drills, screwdrivers and other such devices of possible deconstruction for a chair. Larry could even remember Mick the Nice Caretaker Man who is into Northern Soul Music picking up chairs and taking them places.

"Dear Mick the Nice Caretaker Man who is into Northern Soul Music" wrote Simon

"Please can you take away this most lovely, but unfortunately broken chair…", Larry's heart would have leaped into his mouth had he had one, if it had been possible for a chair to faint Larry was sure he would have done so by now, he was to be taken away, but what would happen to him, oh the misery, oh the devastation, oh the fear.

"…and try to fix it." continued Simon. Larry would have, if at all possible, jumped up and down with excitement and happiness, good old Simon the Happy Librarian.

"If you can't fix it then please kill it and bury it with the others or wherever you can find space." finished Simon with a flourish.

"Ah!" Larry would have thought if it had been possible for a chair to think. "Bugger"

6

Absurd, but interesting to know that
he was still writing even during
what must have been the busiest time
of his life with a baby for the
first time and a big impressive job.

He didn't stay there for long
though. Maybe it was then that
London started to flood from the sea
rising. Or maybe the air quality in
the big city just wasn't good enough
for babies by then, they were still
using oil as fuel in their transport
back then and the cities were choked
by it. From then on SD Downs and
his young and growing family spent
their lives moving ever further
north to higher and cleaner ground.

The next story comes from when he
was living in Oxford. Still in
Britain, Oxford was famous for its
University. And its green and
pleasant rolling hills. Higher
ground see. His wife was really
clever so she got to study in Oxford
and SD Downs got to live there too

and found work in the University libraries.

We're out of the "Old PC Stuff" file now and into the neatly arranged "Story" files on the Mac. "Old PC Stuff" was just one folder with lots of files rammed in it that I've had to go through and sort to figure out what everything is and where it came from.

In the "Story" files everything is arranged, there are folders for "completed" and "Incomplete" stories and each story has its own folder. Some contain several different versions or drafts of the same story, some have art work to go with them and a few have letters from and to publishers about the story and if they are or aren't going to publish it.

SD Downs wasn't a big famous author, yet, he wasn't known by everyone all over the world and he didn't have books in all the libraries. But he was starting to get some of his short stories published here and there in magazines, and local books. I'm sure that would have happened for him, all the signs are there. But these were the end times and civilisation, and publishing, were breaking down.

Some might say that publishing IS civilisation. And that is why what I am doing (what this is) is so important. It might seem a bit extreme, but certainly the language and communication they represent are a big factor in the beginning of civilisation. It could be that was why the end happened, remember I said some of the different countries had their own languages? Well, there were lots of different languages and most people could only speak one or two of them.

Can you imagine how badly they communicated with each other when they didn't even understand or speak the same language? They had to have people called translators, people who could speak two languages, person A would speak to the translator and then the translator would repeat what person A said to person B in a different language.

Imagine the power of the translator,

if they didn't like what someone was saying they could change it. Or if they didn't know the languages well enough they could just get things wrong. Some of the languages had words that couldn't be translated into other languages and when they tried it just came out as something meaning something different. Pretty chaotic.

SD Downs knew all these things about language and translating. When he lived in Hungary teaching his language he had to learn Hungarian so that he could speak to the people around him that weren't in his classes. He spotted very quickly how easily the meanings of words could change and be changed when translating. Also he learned that sometimes people didn't want to understand foreigners even when they were speaking to you in your own language, apparently this was particularly the case with bus drivers in Hungary.

So, SD Downs was already moving north. And to higher ground. Less populated ground. Clearly the CCC was in full swing. The EMP bombs

were still a few years away and the
"Earth Friendly" nuclear war was a
long way off but the place was
starting to become a mess.

As the smaller countries lost all of
their stuff the people from them
tried to leave and get to other
countries that had stuff. Stuff
like food and drink, that their
countries didn't have any more and
were needed for them to stay alive.

Yes, the countries were so obsessed
with getting more stuff that even
when the people around them had got
so little that they couldn't live
anymore the countries with all the
stuff didn't even think about giving
out just a little of their stuff to
help keep those people alive.

Even worse, when the people from the
countries with no stuff turned up at
the countries where all the stuff
had ended up, those countries
wouldn't let them come in. During
my travels I found one of the places
where two countries touched each
other and on the one side was the
remains of all the stuff, all broken
and useless now, though I did find

some good tinned food. No Root Beer though, like I said, rare stuff.

Right next to all that stuff though, on the other side of a line they had drawn on the ground, was just fields and fields of what are just skeletons now. I found some pictures of what that must have been. Huge areas of people living in fields, without houses of any sort, no stuff, no food. All living right next to the line, trying to be let in to the country with all the stuff and that country just saying no and leaving them there until they died.

In a way I suppose it was a sort of justice. That all the people that remained in the final countries, those that were left after the EMP's, the CCC, the "Earth Friendly" Nuclear war, that survived, were then all killed by the horrible disease that they called "The Pandemic".

Back in the olden days, before everything happened, as well as all the electronic stuff that eventually got destroyed by EMP's and then sea rising and so on, they also had lots of chemical stuff that worked for them. Some of it helped to make them healthy and physically strong.

At some point, not long after they'd destroyed all of their electronic stuff, the chemicals that they used to not get ill and die stopped working too. And that's what caused "The Pandemic" which over a really short period of time, a year or two, killed everybody who stayed in the countries. I'm pretty happy that my grandparents joined the Human Race instead of staying in their country. I mean, I wouldn't be here, I wouldn't have even existed if they hadn't.

How did I get this off topic again? SD Downs was traveling north, he was living in Oxford, working in the University library and we were up to the well kept "Story" files on the Mac. Right, yes, he was starting to get published but I'm not presenting anything here that looks like it got published because you might have read that somewhere before. This is all just new stuff, brand new stories that you can't have possibly ever read before.

And this next one is called
"Swerve". In the intro SD Downs
claims it is an old story of his
that he has recently typed up and
finished but, as you've already
seen, SD Downs seemed to like the
old "discovered manuscript" story
device so it's difficult to tell how
true that is.

Also he goes on to almost claim it's
a true story, and we know what we
think about that sort of claim from
him after the werewolf story. I
think this is the solidification of
one of his story telling tropes.

.

Swerve

Word Count: 3224

By SD Downs

Oxford 2025

Intro

This is a really old story. A really really old story.
This story is so old that when I found it in my bottom
drawer I had trouble reading the hand writing. I know
that I wrote it because I know the people in it and that
car journey, that car journey was real. Or at least....
"Most" of what happens next, really happened.

His name was Edward but they called him Trod.
How he became known as Trod is a boring story, it is
enough to know that they called him Trod. He was
the eldest, the most responsible, most sensible of them
all. He was driving. The others in the car, Simon,
Paul and Rob were not as old; they were less
responsible and not so sensible. Trod wasn't there to
look after them, sometimes he even did silly,
humorous things, but he was sensible, he was
responsible and he was reliable. The others… Were
not.

As Trod drove the hundred or so miles to their
holiday destination the others joked, messed around
and laughed. Trod joined in with his friends, but he
didn't throw his rubbish out of the window, that
would have been wrong. Trod didn't reach over from

the back seat to change the music on the car stereo, that could have been dangerous. Trod wore his seat belt, it was the law. They tried to make fun of him, of his music selection, of his driving and of the things that he said. It wasn't nasty stuff, it was just "having fun" and Trod, in his own way, was having fun too. Nobody thought that Trod could be a killer, even though "Contract Killer" was his nickname. He even had a catch phrase: "If you wake up dead, you know who did it!"

As it flew, the pigeon looked about. To its left it could see the sea, it had been able to see the sea for some time now and it thought it was time for a change of scenery. Below it was one of the brightly coloured fast moving things following a big grey snake that disappeared into forever on its right.

They were nearly there now, not quite arrived at their destination but already they'd had adventures and had stories to tell. A few minutes after they had left the motorway the exhaust had fallen off of Trod's car. The others, those in the back, had screamed at him about sparks spraying up from behind his car and the engine had suddenly become loud. Trod had been sensible, he had slowed down, slowly, and pulled to the side of the road.

Trod hadn't worried or panicked as the others had made loud noises and flapped about. The exhaust had been rattling for a couple of weeks; the engine had been getting louder for a few days. Presumably the rattling had cracked the exhaust and now it had broken off completely. It was to be expected, the car wasn't new and Trod had to look after it carefully to keep it going. Trod watched the others as they clambered under the car to inspect the damage and when they began telling him that his car was rubbish, or that maybe it was his driving that was the problem, he stopped them with a steady and clear warning "Aye now!" he bellowed raising his hand. When they continued he turned around with a smile and said, "If that's the way you want it, just remember if you wake up tomorrow morning in the tent and you're dead… You know who did it!" Everybody had laughed.

The broken bit of the exhaust was put inside the car on the laps of the others in the back; they continued on to their campsite the car sounding more like a powerboat. Trod thought about what needed to be done, they needed to get their tents up for the night and then tomorrow he could get the car into a local garage and it could all be fixed while they were relaxing on the beach.

The pigeon was tired. It had been flying for a long time now and it wanted to eat, drink and rest. There hadn't been any fast moving things on the grey snake for a while so it glided down to take a closer look at it. There was often food to be found on a grey snake. It landed near a brown wet patch. It smelled good, you had to be careful of the jagged sharp bits, they weren't food, but the sticky liquid was very good, it had drunk it before. The pigeon walked casually over to the middle of the road and began to drink the beer that had leaked out of the smashed beer bottle.

Trod drove on as the light began to fade, the laughter and the fooling around continuing around him inside the car. Trod was sensible, he concentrated on his

driving. He ignored their pleas to speed up and get

them there before it got dark, it was a waste of fuel

and they just wanted to hear the engine roar because it

was comical coming from his little Fiat Uno. They

could put the tents up by the light from the car's

headlamps if necessary, better to arrive safely than

not at all.

The pigeon drank.

Trod drove.

"Hey look! A pigeon!"

"Go on Trod, hit it"

"Yeah Trod, Trod's gonna kill it!"

"You'll never hit it, you always miss pigeons even if

you try to hit them. Just when you think WHOOA!"

"YEAH!"

"Did you see that!"

"There was, like, a cloud of feathers"

"I can't believe you actually managed to hit it!"

"Trod!"

"Trod!"

"Trod!"

Sensible, responsible, reliable.

"I didn't aim at it. I drove straight, I didn't swerve!
It says it in the highway code, you shouldn't over
react to animals in the road, don't risk doing an
emergency stop or swerving to save an animal on the
road because it could cause an accident that could
injure or kill a human. I didn't aim at it, I drove

straight. I'm not going to risk a human life for a pigeon. I didn't kill it!"

Some how, as the front wheel of the car had run over the pigeon it had flung it backwards at the back wheel which had then stapled the pigeon to the road as it passed over it. The pigeon was drunk, it had tasted a little of the beer and then greedily gobbled all that it could find. By the time the car came into view the pigeon was drunkenly pecking ineffectively at the sticky road surface.

As the noise of the car disappeared into the distance the pigeon drunkenly realised that it was lying on its back held in place by its left wing which appeared to be glued to the road now, it was quite stuck. The pigeon's alcohol soaked brain had got quite jumbled by the ride around the front wheel but the pain all about its body was slowly breaking through the confusion. Soon the pain grew so that it was everything in the pigeons world, it couldn't remember a time before the pain and every heart beat seemed to double the agony. Crushed, shattered bone, ripped, torn flesh. Again and again the pigeon followed its natural instinct to try and roll over and stand up only to be rewarded with a small crack and a sharp stab of pain that was soon lost in the noise of all the other pain.

Panic began to creep in around the edges of the pain, the pigeon shifted its weight from left to the right and again and again, it started to flap its right wing as the pain began to numb at its extremities and centre in on its heart. As the pigeon began to lose heart in its escape attempts there was a wet snap and the pigeon rolled away from its left wing, which stayed stuck to the road. The pigeon rolled several times before coming to rest on its back once more. The throbbing pain from around its body had gone now, there was just a sharp pulsing pain coming from its heart. The stabbing pain cleared the pigeon's head and its eyes were able to focus once more. They focused on the trail of red from its flattened wing leading to where it lay now. Free at last.

The pigeon rolled to its right to stand up but instantly overbalanced due to the missing wing and, spinning like a ballerina, fell to the floor once more. Confusion, pain, dizziness and a sick feeling washed over the pigeon. That last could well have been the alcohol; it had felt it before when it had drunk the brown sticky. Just five minutes after starting the binge drinking the pigeon was beginning to sober up and it had one hell of a bad hangover.

The pigeon weakly flapped its right wing and waggled its legs, to little affect other than wobbling it about a bit. It paused and then gradually pressed onto the road with its one remaining wing until it had half pushed itself upright. With a combination of two wobbly legs and a wing tip it managed to get into an almost standing position where it paused to take in the situation. Its left wing was behind it, still stuck to the ground, whilst in front of it the pigeon could see the brown sticky patch it had been supping at minutes ago. It looked at the brown patch longingly; it could really do with some more of that. The pulse of the stabbing pain in its heart had slowed and in between the beats there was a numbness that the pigeon was happy with. It made it feel sleepy and comfortable. That brown patch was calling though, a little drink from there could well help sort it out, perhaps even get rid of the pain all together. If the pain went away, thought the pigeon, it could gather the energy to get going and fly again.

A light drizzle began to fall, creating a haziness to everything the pigeon could see. It opened its beak to let water fall in. A few small drops fell in but they seemed to dry up before the pigeon could swallow them. They tasted warm and metallic in its mouth. Bracing itself mentally for the pain, the pigeon flapped its right wing and moved its legs like it was running. The flapping became more frantic as it felt its feet moving along the ground, paddling for all it was worth. It shot forwards quickly towards the brown sticky patch but was almost instantly slowing, its feet were soon dragging and its wing flaps became mechanical and sporadic until it collapsed on its front the pigeon's beak inches from the edge of the brown patch.

The pigeon concentrated on breathing and tried to ignore its body. For half an hour or more the pigeon concentrated on breathing and didn't try to move its body at all. The light hazy rain turned into proper rain drops which splashed about the pigeons head, water got into its beak and slipped down its throat slowly reviving it a little from its meditative slumber. The pigeon angled its head to let more water fall into its partly open beak, its eyes followed a stream of lightly red stained water back to its origin, the pigeons flattened left wing. It didn't seem very far away, the pigeon was sure it had moved more than that, but there it was. It looked back in front of it to see that the rain was washing the brown patch away. The edge of it, which had been inches away, was now almost half a metre away. The pigeon closed its eyes and lifted its open beak to the sky, letting in as much rainwater as possible, gulping greedily at it.

Refreshed by the water the pigeon's heart seemed to pick up speed and strength, even the stabbing pain had dulled to a numb ache now. The pigeon thought of where it should go onto now. Some place green, it thought, with no humans and no grey snake, no fast moving big things. As it thought of this utopian new homeland a deep rumble followed a flash of light onto the pigeon and its world was once again turned upside down.

The driver of the blue van didn't even feel the bump, he was busy wiping at the steamed up windscreen whilst trying to see the road ahead through the downpour.

Although hit square on by the front wheel of the van the pigeon didn't get flattened to the road, instead it took another ride around a front wheel and got flung forwards, this time, landing ahead of the van in the centre of the road on the white line. The van continued past, the wind of its passing ruffling the wet messed up feathers of the now dead bird. It lay around 12 metres from the broken bottle, the only indicator left now of the spilt beer it had dined on earlier. Face down, its left side was split open and internal organs poked out, a small fading trickle of blood mixed with the rain water flowing down the road after the blue van. Though dead in the head, the bird's wing twitched once, then twice and its feet clenched and unclenched. Then the only movement was that caused by the rain as it hit the dead birds feathers and splashed.

Trod was happy, they had arrived at the campsite safely, it was just the other side of the village that they had gone through right after hitting the pigeon. Hitting the pigeon had been an accident, he hadn't aimed at it, he had driven straight, he was sure of it. They had pitched their tents by the light of the car's headlamps, it was drizzling but they managed to get the tents up before it had started to rain properly. After a quick snack they had walked back into the village in search of a pub that would serve them all or at least let Trod, who was the only one legally old enough, buy a round of drinks and take it to them at a table outside or something. Rob said that he'd seen one called "The Dog and Duck" as they'd entered the village so they followed his lead.

The others had teased him about being a "pigeon murderer" and had demanded to know who had taken out a contract on the pigeon's life. They'd even had a pretend argument about who would sleep in the same tent as the pigeon killer, as though they were afraid one of them might be next. Trod had played along, alternately protesting his innocence and then making mock death threats when they wouldn't leave it alone. They were definitely on holiday now; they'd arrived and were on their way to a pub.

Trod hadn't really been making note of where Rob was leading them, even as they exited the village following the main road that they'd driven in on. He certainly had no idea they were walking on the same road as the one he'd hit the pigeon on. Not until he heard "Whoa, shit! Look at that"

"Urgh! That is gross. Trod, look what you did!"

"Oh man, that is sick."

Trod looked at what the others had walked ahead to gather around, a shudder of disgust running through him as he realised what it must be. "You stapled its wing to the road and then it crawled around with its insides leaking out. You freaking mad man. You murderer!" The accusation hung in the air for a few seconds. Before the others began again more quietly. "I bet it was in pain for hours, cursing you Trod."

"Don't be silly," said Trod "We haven't been here for hours, besides it probably died really quickly. It couldn't have survived for long, look at it!"

"You murderer. You tortured your victim beyond belief until it died and you don't even care about the pain it was in. I bet you enjoyed thinking about it being in pain. Turn you on did it?"

"Yeah Trod, do you get a thrill from killing?"

Trod was becoming unsure about where the line between a joke and reality was, were they really upset at the dead pigeon or was this still friendly joshing from the lads?

"It's only a pigeon, it's like a goldfish, it probably doesn't remember one minute to the next and doesn't feel pain." Trod paused a little and then added

"You're talking like I did this deliberately."

"You did!" the others all chorused.

"Oh shut up! No I didn't, it was on the other side of the road and I drove straight and it moved and flew into the front of my car. If anything, it hit me! If I'd aimed at it, if I'd swerved to hit it I'd understand the fuss but I didn't, I didn't try to kill it. I'm not a killer. It just happened. But... It is dead, and that is because I was here so I suppose. In a way, it is sort of my fault." The others were silent "Look, I am sorry the bird is dead," pleaded Trod. Rob smiled and said, "Yeah, sure you are." Simon nodded and Paul smiled and headed on towards the pub. Simon followed leaving Trod and Rob looking at each other across the dead pigeon in the middle of the road.

"I'm sorry the pigeon suffered an hour of agony.

Rob."

Rob looked up from the dead pigeon to look at Trod. Something about the last word wasn't right. Trod sounded odd. Rob was concentrating so hard on the strange look in Trod's eyes that he didn't even feel the blade of the knife as it entered his body, not for a few seconds. It entered his body just below his heart and sliced into it as it was withdrawn. Rob didn't make a sound as he slumped to the ground until the wet slap of his face hitting the concrete.

Though on a slightly different scale, Trod told a very similar story about Rob as he had about the pigeon. He had done everything by the book. When a knife wielding "mugger" (who nobody else ever saw) had appeared behind himself and Rob, as the others walked on towards the pub, Trod had handed over his wallet without arguing but Rob had refused. That's against the advice given by the police when dealing with weapon wielding muggers. A scuffle had started and Rob had been stabbed. So the story went, as Trod told it. Trod had called for the police and an ambulance but by the time they had arrived Rob was already dead.

If somebody hadn't believed his story, if they had checked a little harder, maybe somebody would have been able to tell that Rob hadn't died from the stab wound, though it was a fatal wound and would have killed him eventually. And if they had been able to tell that Rob had died from suffocation and not from the stab wound then maybe Trod would have had some more explaining to do, a little more story to tell.

He certainly couldn't have told them the truth that Rob simply wasn't dying quickly enough, so Trod had gently pinched his nose and firmly covered his mouth until he had stopped struggling. No, he'd have had to come up with something special to get out of that one. If anybody had checked and been able to tell.

7

That one has got some gruesome bits. You've had one that was sort of a parody of gothic horror before but I think "Swerve" might fall into the "horror" category proper, what do you think? Thriller? I suppose it has a twist, could that make it a murder mystery? To begin with SD Downs appears to have enjoyed "genre" fiction and many of his earlier short stories seem to be him learning a new genre, or at least trying it out.

Later on, and as his works got bigger, he dips into multiple genres in each work and sometimes I think he deliberately begins in one genre, following the rules and conventions and then wilfully breaks out of that genre into a completely different one. But I'll talk more of his "bigger works" later on. Oh yes, more twists and plot turns to come.

Once the sea rise really started to bite, SD Downs and family moved

right in to the centre of Britain,
to the place furthest from the sea.
Even back then Britain was a fairly
small island (now, what's left of
what was, is just a collection of
hundreds of tiny islands that were
once hill and mountain peaks) so
that didn't get him too far away.
But enough to feel safe for a while.

Once ensconced into their safe place
SD Downs really started to get down
to work. He got a new computer (the
one I am using right now actually)
and, as you might expect from a
librarian, he started to order and
keep his work neatly and
methodically. It's really been much
easier for me to sort through stuff
from this period onwards.

The problem for us is that he
started to get noticed. And
published. That's the real sticky
point. Once all the electrical
stuff started getting broken books
(physical, hard copy, made from
paper books) made a come back. Big
time. They became, as well you
know, the main form of passive
entertainment. There's no video
anymore, all the screens and players

are broken.

I was amazed at finding some on
here, but this is the first working
computer I've ever found. The area
where my parents had me and I grew
up had a functioning TV monitor in
their library but they didn't have
any videos on it. It was hooked up
to a camera and it showed a live
feed of whatever was in front of the
camera. I used to watch it
sometimes trying to imagine what it
would have been like to see things
that weren't actually happening just
around the corner or that were
completely made up even.

The films on here are mind blowing.
Oh, you can tell they aren't real,
but to see somebody else's ideas and
stories being shown visually is just
stunning. And the music, there is
so much music on this computer,
hundreds of hours of it. I've been
here months now and every day I
listen to some of the music and I'm
not even half way through everything
that is on here.

But books is where it's really at
now. But with no new ones being

made all the ones from before the
end are wearing out, each year there
are fewer and fewer of them. The
stories that we have are getting old
and well know. And lost. This is
why what I am doing is so important,
why SD Downs is so important.

Yes, by this period he was getting
published and I've seen some of his
works published and printed and on
paper in books and magazines. They
aren't new, you may have seen them,
you probably know them. Though he
hardly ever used his name, so you
don't know him. As far as I have
been able to tell, and I've done a
lot of work on this, his fake names
always had the same initials as him.
SD.

If you look through some of your
short story collections and
magazines with stories in you'll
find authors with the initials SD.
They won't all be him, in fact most
of them won't be, but some of the
time, if it's an SD it's SD Downs.
I've seen Steven Downy, Simone
Dawson, Stephen Duffy, Susan Dunn,
Sharon Dexter and more that have
stories published that I've found

the files for on this computer from
original first draft through
iterations to the final published
article.

There are other authors I have
spotted that have stories published
that SD Downs has very similar ideas
and notes about in an "Ideas" file
(in the old PC files ideas were kept
in a file marked "Notes and
Candles") that I can't prove to be
him, but at least a few of them
could very well be. Sharon
Dorchester, Scott Dempsy, Sarah
Dunant, Sam Devine, Sara Douglass
and now you are starting to see.
You do know SD Downs, no doubt you
have probably read some of his work
already.

But this is all new. As he became
more popular he became more
published and while you may have
read some of his work there is more
that you haven't. More that wasn't
published or that was published
electronically. That was a big
thing back then. Everyone was
reading on their electronic devices,
they had them with them at all
times. Of course, many of his

stories that were published
electronically were never printed on
paper and were lost. Until now!

SD Downs, under his many fake names,
was winning prizes (and fans) by
this stage. Winning prizes often
included getting published in a book
or a magazine so many of his prize
winning stories are knocking about
in print out there in the world.
This next story is a rare one in
that it was prize winning but for an
electronic only publication, so it
was never mass printed on paper for
the public, only displayed
electronically.

I found a print out of it hidden
under a draw in the study he created
in the loft of a house he and his
family lived in on top of a hill on
the edge of a forrest. I'm used to
hunting around for hidden things in
houses and remains of houses. We
all are. By now most places have
been ransacked at least once if not
more often, so the only way you are
going to find something is when it
has been hidden or lost.

In Oxford SD Downs had a shed that

he worked in. There's nothing left
of that now and, at first, I had
guessed he might have continued his
study in a shed trend at this house.
There was no shed or shed remains
but what of a flimsy wooden shed
would I expect to find still intact
now? There was the remains of a
garage. A well kept garage situated
in the back garden. It had the
scraggy remains of a carpet on the
floor and a battered old filing
cabinet in the corner at the back.

I'd had luck with filing cabinets in
Hungary twice and once in London too
(that one was under water and a
right adventure it was finding it)
but this one had been all but
completely cleared out. All that I
found was some rotted cloth that had
once been a shirt, some picture
frames with faded to nothing
pictures in them and empty hanging
file dividers. I assumed it had
been his study but that it had been
totally cleared out during, what I
would soon find out was to be, his
final move.

Then I found the loft study,
pristine and complete, but once

again completely cleared out. It
was a real hidden treasure. There
were no stairs up into the loft and
the ladder, that must have been his
method of getting in, was broken.
As I fashioned a way in by piling
rubble high enough for me to climb
into the hatch in the ceiling, for
that was all that the entrance was,
I was in no way expecting or even
hoping for what I was about to find.

The loft had been comfortably
converted into a writing study.
Fitted carpets, that even now were
in no bad shape, a beautiful large
wooden desk with filing cabinet
drawers had been built into the far
end of the loft away from the hatch.
There was no chair left, no windows
to let in light but the roof was
intact and other than a fine
covering of dust and a modest amount
of cobwebs the place was as it had
been left.

I suspect the occupants following on
from SD Downs and his family had not
made it up into the loft. It wasn't
usual to find a usable space there,
none of the surrounding houses had
anything other than boxes of junk in

theirs, if that.

It has become my habit to remove
drawers to check for things that may
have fallen out and remained hidden
but while this manuscript was indeed
hidden, there was nothing accidental
about it, as the cover note
explained in his very own hand:

In your hands you now hold the
long lost story of a famous writer.
At least that's the plan. I lived in
this house before you and I wrote
this story here. I shall never
publish it, and I have shown it to
no one. If I do go on to become a
famous author (and that is my
intention) then what you now hold
in your hands will be the lost story
of SD Downs, world wide best
seller. Imagine its worth. The
longer you hang on to it, keeping it

secret, the more it will be worth.

Or, maybe, I'll never get anything published and you'll never have heard of me, in which case you hold nothing more than a few minutes light entertainment and the delusions of a mad man. Either way you enjoy it and choose to do with it whatever you will.

SD Downs

And so, this is how I know that none of you have ever read this before, please may I present to you, the long lost (though actually written before many of his other published works) story titled "I Killed a Frog" by SD Downs:

The long lost:

I Killed a Frog

Word Count: 2695

By SD Downs

Cannock Chase 2032

"Urgh! Look Mommy!"

The little girl stood and pointed.

"What is it d… Urgh! Get away from that dear, it's

disgusting!"

Came Mommy's distressed reply.

"What is it Mommy, what is it?"

"I have no idea sweet heart, but it looks very dirty and

is certainly nothing that you should go near, my

dear."

The sentence was final and with a little tug on her

hand the daughter and mother moved on, mother

moving purposefully, daughter slightly dragging

behind trotting to keep up.

Back on the pavement where the little girl had

shrieked and the mother had been revolted, lay a quite

flat, quite dirty, very dead frog. It probably wasn't

old, for a frog, but as an object, which it had now become, it was starting to look worn and very much on its way out. It was flattened, like an old piece of chewing gum stuck to the road, though possibly the frog was a little less smooth. Any blood that had been spilled was dried up now and its skin was dry, dirt covered and dusty.

I had stood back as the scene with the little girl and mom had played out. I'd pretended to be really interested in the arrangement of envelopes in the post office shop window, a tough sell but one I thought I had succeeded at. Of course, all my attention had actually been on the little girl, the mom and the frog. I knew what they were looking at from the very first "Urgh!" and that was what necessitated my pretending to look at an envelope display. I knew it

was a dead frog and I would have gladly told the little
girl if only she had asked me and not her mother.

Maybe, if I had told this little girl, that the splat on the
pavement, the dirty mess her mother didn't want her
going near, had once been a living, breathing,
hopping creature, she wouldn't have believed me.
Maybe she would have, maybe she would have been
grossed out by it, I'm pretty sure she wouldn't have
looked back at me and smiled as I made a funny face
whilst she walked away, which is what she (and I) did
next. I imagine if I had told her that the dirty mess
was a dead frog and it was there because I had killed
it, she would have given me a very different look.
She might even have been the one dragging her
mother away from me instead of the other way
around.

I killed the frog last Tuesday. There is and was nothing special about last Tuesday. Not really. I don't think there was anything special about the frog either, dead or alive. To be honest, I hadn't spent anytime thinking about that frog, not even as I killed it or afterwards as my drunken mates cheered and booed my action. Not a thought, until now. I'd just been walking along on my way to get a few supplies. A few of us are on a camping holiday together, my brother and I and a couple of mates. I'd woken up fancying a cooked breakfast this morning and seeing as nobody else was awake I'd got dressed and was walking into the near by village to buy some bacon and eggs, perhaps even some mushrooms and / or black pudding if they had any.

I wasn't taking any notice of the woman and girl in

front of me (other than noticing what a nice bum the lady had as she walked in front of me. Hey, I'm a teenager, it's what we do ;0) until the little girl had made her yelp of discovery. As soon as she made the noise the memory clicked into my mind and I instinctively knew exactly what she had seen. Instantly I sought to hide my face, call it irrational guilt, I knew there was no way they could connect what they were looking at with me but for whatever reason my brain had decided 'Hide!' was the logical course of action to take. Hence my sudden interest in envelopes, the post office shop being the only thing I could possibly be looking at other than the couple (and dead frog) in front of me.

Although my eyes were locked in the direction of the display of 3 sizes of envelope (£1 for a packet £1:75

for 2 packets. No word on how many envelops in a packet.) they were focused upon the little girl, thanks to the reflection in the window. As soon as the mother started to tug the little girl along I turned my head and stood next to the post office shop window watching them walk away. The little girl skittered at first to keep up before relaxing into a walk then skip to catch up medley. Back into a rhythm she had turned her head for another look at the interesting splat and had noticed me, staring openly at me as only children can do. I stuck out my tongue, went cross eyed and then grinned stupidly at her whilst winking. It was something I could remember my dad doing to me; I thought I'd give it a go. The girl giggled and turned her head around to once more skip and catch up with her mother.

Other than the little girl and mother there was nobody else around, so now I was alone with my envelope display and flattened dead frog. Or so I had thought. The woman behind the counter inside the post office shop had noticed outside her window and was giving me a look. I wasn't sure what kind of a look it was but I didn't want it developing so I headed on my way, back on track for my plan of a cooked breakfast. Five, maybe six paces got me to within a leap of the flattened dead frog, and here my stride hesitated, slowed and then stopped completely.

Right next to the dead frog, I could see how dirty and nasty it looked now. It reminded me of a half cooked pancake that has been dropped during the flip and scraped back into the pan, now all covered in dirt and dust from the floor.

Tuesday was four nights ago, so that little fellow was doing well to still be sticking around. Normally dead animals disappear much quicker than that, a run over cat on my route to school had been pretty much erased within two days, nothing but a patch of dirty fur that could have been a bit of rug in the gutter of the road. Even that had been gone by the third day.

If I had to go into a full CSI / Bones type investigation into the body at the crime scene I'd guess the frog had been run over, possibly by a pram or pushchair. It had two much flatter stripes running through its already fairly flattened body. It had a more noticeable frog shaped form than the dead cat had had cat shaped form on its second morning, and this frog was on morning number 4. "You certainly have sticking power…" I mumbled the 'dad level' joke, the words hitting my lips at the same time they hit my brain. I instantly regretted it. Crap joke. Plus, I'm talking to myself here, how mad is that. A little shouting at the TV to tell the ref how rubbish he is being whilst watching football is pretty much socially acceptable (almost mandatory within my peer group) but mumbling at a frog, dead or alive… Pretty dumb.

Maybe the frog had stuck so well to the ground because of its method of demise. I'm not that strong, but then the frog is comparatively very weak next me. And likely less dense than a bouncy ball.

Walking back to our campsite from the beach moderately early one night (about 1am or something) we were all fairly well drunk. I'd had a couple of bottles of cider, three cans of super strength lager and a mouth full or two of vodka. I was drunk, but much less so than my brother, Paul, or Rob, who were the older two of our group of four. It was they who had purchased the alcohol, my brother being of age and Rob distinctly looking like he might be, more so than Paul at least, even though he had a few months to go yet. They'd gone for vodka and had then stolen a can of my cider to remove the taste of vodka, of which they were not fans, before tucking into some of Andrew's lager. This combination had them stumbling along well out of it and laughing at pretty much anything.

We'd gone to the beach to build a campfire and drink, but upon finding little driftwood with which to build a fire had, in the end, just drunk. By the time we had finished all our liquids we'd walked a fair way along the beach and decided that it would be quicker to climb up the beach wall and through a field or two to get back to the campsite. After the first field we hit a road and guessing that it would take us to the campsite we had followed it.

By the time we entered the village Andrew had sobered up enough to be trying to stop Paul and Rob from stumbling about in the road, as he was convinced they were going to get run over. They were so drunk, and so much bigger than him, that they were just swearing at him as they stumbled forever back into the middle of the road as he tried to push them onto the path. Paul didn't know it, but he was about five minutes away from being sick, if we'd been near a hospital I'm certain someone would have said something about alcohol poisoning.

Whilst this little pantomime was going on I was still drunk enough to think running around in the road was funny, making Andrew shout even more, but not drunk enough not to be aware, at least, of where the path was, were it to be needed. And then it was spotted. I don't remember if it was me or one of the others (drunk is drunk) but one of us shouted "Hey! Look at that!" There followed a drunken 3 way conversation

"What the fucks that?"

"Eh? What?"

"He's seen something."

"Look at that!"

"Bloody 'ell, wha's that?"

"Argh!"

"Argh!"

"Argh!"

"Argh!"

The four exclamations all came at the same time as the object of attention suddenly jumped. A good, high, long jump. There was silence and then it jumped again. As it landed on the road, in the darkness, it blended in and was invisible. It hopped again and I realised I'd been looking a few inches in the wrong direction and suddenly I had decided that we must catch this creature. I dived at it; it felt like a professional goalkeepers majestic stretched dive for that penalty shot into the bottom left corner, but I have scrapes and bruises that claim it was a badly tumbled landing.

Even so, I had managed to get my hands over the frog and I felt as it tried to leap again only to bang its head on my hands. I flattened my hands until they pinned the frog firmly to the floor and then I curled my right hand to clasp it in my fist. I was still lying face first on the floor in the middle of the road at this point and Andrew was going mental because he was convinced a car was about to come and run me over. Rob was laughing, cracking up at my drunken fall, whilst Paul was oddly quiet. None of them realised, at this point, that I'd actually caught the frog.

Slowly, I got to my feet whilst keeping hold of the frog in my hand. There was a bit of a stumble and I was drunk enough that I should have fallen back down, I needed my right hand to straighten myself and I should have released the frog to save my face from the concrete of the road, but I didn't, I kept hold of that frog and took the road to the side of my face like a beaten boxer going down for the count and knowing it. I think it was Rob who realised then that I'd actually got the frog. He rushed over to help me up and take a look, pulling my arm towards Paul to show him I'd got the frog. Paul wasn't too interested, he was in a dark place of his own by then, he mumbled "yeah, cool" before waving it away out of his face.

All this time Andrew was still shouting, about being in the road, about the frog and then Rob decided to start shouting back at him. Paul had sat down cross-legged right on the dotted white line in the middle of the road. I guess he about knew by then that he was going to vomit. I stood, gently swaying, watching Rob and Andrew argue. As far as I could tell Andrew was angry because we were drunk and acting like idiots who were going to get themselves run over and

Rob was angry because Andrew was a lot smaller than him, was a light weight, had thrown most of his lager away and should just stop being such a sissy.

I could see both points of view but the argument, and the frog, left my mind as Paul started to hurl his stuff. It was a real pumping fountain of liquid spew that had us all quiet instantly. Andrew sat on the curb, slightly uphill from the flow while Rob walked over to Paul and crouched down, probably just within the splash back area, to loudly say words to Paul like he was a deaf old man. "You OK mate? Yeah go on mate, get it all out. That feeling better?"

In between gulps for air Paul managed to express an extreme interest in getting a drink of water to swill his mouth out with. We were a few hundred metres from the campsite and Rob decided he'd jog there to get his mate some water. He was all over the shop and I could see he was going to end up arse over tit before he got anywhere near our tent so I decided that I could do the job quicker and better.

The frog was a last second thought, if any thought was involved at all. A boost of adrenaline hit me as I made the decision that I was going to run for the water, and I leaped into the air bringing my frog bearing hand above my head and then hurling it at the floor, releasing the frog, as I began my sprint. It landed with a loud smacking noise and without a bounce of any sort. It didn't hop or even twitch now that its freedom had been returned.

"Oh, what did you do that for, you twat!" said

Andrew, in a disgusted voice, but I was running by then, full on sprinting, past Rob and by the time Andrew had finished calling me a twat I was well on my way towards remedying my brothers situation. Nobody hates the taste of vomit more than me, so all sympathy for the one having to taste it.

There was a small attempt to label me a frog murderer the next morning, but Rob wasn't involved so it didn't stick. Apart from that, not a thought for the frog I had killed had entered my mind. Until now. "I don't know what you're sticking around for..." another mumbled, very poor, joke from me and I walked on towards the village shop, on my way to sort out that cooked breakfast dream of mine.

I didn't notice the frog on my way back, or even think

of it again as I cooked the bacon, egg and black

pudding back at the tent.

8

I suspect, had that been published years after a very successful and well published SD Downs had died, it would have been a bit of a disappointment. An early short story by someone famous for their novels, not huge news. Unless…

He obviously held that story and the note that he had left with it in his head. Throughout his work afterwards there are nods to the story, the characters show up in the background, there are oblique and outright blatant references to it. It's all through his work, hiding in it from here on out.

I think his plan was to have all of his fans talking about it, discussing it.

"What's with SD Downs and all his references to dead frogs?"

"Is this "missing story" really real?"

"Why do these characters keep turning up in the background?"

"Seriously, what is it with SD Downs and dead frogs?"

It's a neat idea. Create a mystery, a myth, a legend and then at some point it is revealed, at last, the truth! Probably still a disappointment upon publication, but I love the idea of what it would do to fans for all the time before it was discovered.

Once the rise of the ocean level really started to hit, the high ground in the middle of Britain got really crowded really quick. SD Downs and his family moved on further north to the islands of what was left of Scotland, the northern part of Britain.

And that's where I am now, and where SD Downs is too and his family. Or, at least, their resting place. That should come as no surprise, I haven't tried to hide that he's dead, I'm not a talented author springing twists and turns on you in an intricately convoluted plot. I'm not an author at all, I am merely an introducer, introducing SD Downs to the world.

Here are some true facts about SD Downs that I have found out and verified during my research:

1. He once made a Hungarian Army Officer cry, just by talking to him.

2. He once got to the finals of both a freestyle and breast stroke swimming race but was disqualified from both. In the breast stroke he did freestyle and in the freestyle he did breast stroke. Despite doing the wrong stroke he won both races.

3. He captained a Cricket team and a Football team for a prestigious Oxford University College even though he didn't study there. He took the football team to an immigration detention centre to play against the foreign prisoners to cheer them up.

4. At the age of 50 he taught himself how to make solar panels without any electronic parts.

5. He once moved a High School Library into a girls toilet.

6. His best subject at school was history. He won a prestigious prize for his final results in the subject.

7. He once rescued the life of an American (one of the last countries left standing) spy who had been captured by the Serbian (small country, one of the first to end being a country) military.

8. As well as English he also spoke Hungarian, as did his wife, which was considered one of the hardest languages for a native English speaker to learn. They used it to communicate with each other secretly when needed.

9.He never killed a frog. Or did he…?

In his longer work SD Downs often
has a list or two in his stories,
but they seem to have been something
that he did when he was older.
There aren't many in his short
fiction.

This next (and last, for now...)
short story has two lists in it
though, making it pretty rare. It's
another prize winning short story
that I've found that wasn't
published anywhere. At least not
physically, it may have been
published on a digital format but it
was written right before the EMP's
started so even if it was, not many
people would have had time to have
read it.

Lists seem to have been part of his
thought process, I found lots of
them in the notes he kept when
writing his novels. He didn't
always have notes before he wrote,
or at least I've seen some novels
that just have a first draft and a
final draft with no other files
along side them.

He only wrote two works that were
non-fiction. One was his account of

"the end" and how he and his family survived it and lived. It's actually quite story like in the way he tells it but after all my research I am inclined to believe his introduction to that one where he states it is the true and accurate account of his life.

The other is a list of how he thought the world should be. It's fairly short and some of it doesn't make much sense, a lot of it is to do with "money" which is something they used when transferring "ownership" of stuff from one person (or a group of people) to another. I don't really understand all of that but then I don't understand the whole "money" thing and I suspect none of you will.

There is quite a bit that does make sense though and some of it describes how life is for us now. He predicted how important books are and how they would slowly start to disappear. He wrote that things like food and water, power, education, communication and sheltered places to live in should be equally and freely (that means

without the need for "money")
available to everyone.

He didn't suggest getting rid of
"money", which we must have done at
some point because we don't have it
now and never did while I've been
alive. He did correctly predicted
that countries should end and all
the people left on the planet should
become one nation under the name
Humans, yes he even got the name
right and this was way before we
started using it.

If this goes well and I actually
manage to get it done and made into
a new book that's in your hands now
and you're reading it, then I might
have to get that "How Life Should
Be" non-fiction book printed too.
Although it will have to wait until
after I get some of the stories done
first.

Talking of stories, look at me
nattering on again, here is that
final short story, the prize winning
previously unpublished one. It is
called "Autism Killing Me", you'll
be able to figure out what "Autism"
is (you probably already have from

some of the previous stories) from the story.

It seems odd that so few people had brains that worked like that back then, and life was so hard for those that did. We probably see it as a description of some of the things that make us Human, but back then it was seen as a problem or divergent from being human.

Weird how far we have evolved but then I guess back then there were so many people about it just wasn't possible for them to evolve, it was too crowded and divided. And they just did so many stupid things, I guess a lot of the people must have just been stupid. How else can you explain destroying the planet and continuing to go on destroying the planet even when you can see that what you are doing is destroying the planet that you are sat right on top of.

Nattering again, sorry. Here's the story and hang around afterwards I have a few closing words to add. A sort of "exciting announcement" actually.

Autism Killing Me

Word Count: 2032

By SD Downs

Scotland 2040

Intro

When asked by the myriad of "professionals" who pop in and out of our lives, mostly randomly and seemingly with little purpose, what our main concerns are with our severely non-verbal classic autistic 8 year old we invariably say: Making sure he doesn't get himself killed or seriously harmed. This story is about our second most concern, the one that has gone unspoken but is very real, lurking there in the background...

The main thought that went through Dan's mind, as he quickly began to bleed to death, was that if he did die, there would be nobody supervising John. Even when John was under strict supervision he could still get into all sorts of mischief. At school John had one to one supervision, two to one if they went out on a trip and if they were going anywhere overnight chances were he or Susan would have to fetch him home for the night part. Even with all that, John consistently managed to escape from his class room, he'd even got out of the playground a few times, something Dan and Susan had warned them he would do when they first visited the school. He also broke stuff, made big messes, hit and hurt himself and others. About once a week he'd come home in his P.E. kit as he'd just made too much of a mess of himself.

The thing was, telling people, even professionals, that John was Autistic just didn't prepare them for him. The word Autistic covers such a whole load of behaviors with an infinite number of combinations and strengths; that's where the whole "Autistic Spectrum Disorder" phrase came from. John had little, medium and massive sized dots all over the spectrum, if you can think of it as a visual graph. The best Dan could do, and he was aware this didn't make him sound like the caring, loving dad he tried to be, was to ask people to imagine they had a semi trained Chimpanzee in their house.

It's not really what John was like but it would probably create the same sort of mess and destruction plus, Dan imagined, eventually a chimp would want to run off and find some distant trees to play in rather than stay safe and secure in the house. At times this appeared to be what John wanted to do. Certainly whenever he and Susan took John on his own to the zoo (a special and rare treat for him; finding a baby sitter for their other two kids, not without problems themselves, was never easy) Dan or Susan would at some point make the comment that John looked like he just wanted to get inside one of the ape enclosures and play.

10 Things about John, which are similar to having a semi-trained Chimpanzee in the house:

1.   They think throwing their food around is fun, and food found on the floor from a few days ago is still fine to eat.
2.   Throwing and / or smearing the surroundings with poo is fun.

3.   *Putting stuff down the loo is fun. Not poo, but toys, mobile phones anything that looks important etc.*

4.   *Loo rolls exist to be unwound.*

5.   *They both like climbing and are very good at it.*

6.   *They don't talk but might one day be taught how to use some basic sign language and noises.*

7.   *They don't understand the need for clothes and happily run around naked.*

8.   *They need a great deal of exercise and time to run around outside.*

9.   *They have feelings and moods.*

10. *They will both quickly grow out of being small and cute and get stronger and bigger. As adolescents they will be a nightmare and as adults they will be considered scary by some.*

4 Things about John, which aren't similar to having a semi-trained Chimpanzee in the house:

1.   *John <u>could</u> physically talk, he has so far just chosen not to, mainly because he doesn't see the point of it. Or any two-way communication really.*

2.   *John is more intelligent and has impressive problem solving abilities. Abilities he mainly uses*

*to find ways of getting at stuff he wants that other
people don't want him to have.*
3. *John has high expectations of the world around
him and gets extremely frustrated when the world
fails to bend to his will.*
4. *You could probably toilet train a Chimpanzee.
John has yet to show any signs of this ability.*

Dan shifted his weight, as slowly and carefully as he
could, to try and roll himself over onto his side so that
he could see what John was doing. It was a stupid
thing to do, the third stupid thing Dan had done in
less than a minute; as he went from being on his back,
with the messy stab wound in his stomach pointing
upwards, to being on his side, the stab wound tipped
sideways, the affect was like tipping over a bottle.
Liquid glugged out of the wound as it gaped open.

The puddle on the floor was bigger than Dan now, and spreading fast. John had stabbed Dan with the big kitchen knife probably less than 30 seconds ago, maybe even less than 20. Dan couldn't see John, he had left the kitchen, and he couldn't hear him either.

There was no malice in John's action of stabbing Dan. John wasn't capable of malice probably, possibly. He'd once thrown a frog, and Dan was pretty sure it had died, he hadn't done it out of anger or frustration, he'd just been so excited to be holding it. When John had picked up the knife Dan had panicked and shouted "No!" lunging towards him to try and grab the knife, which was the first stupid thing Dan had done. When John had something you wanted back the best way to get it was to stand still, put out your hand palm up and very calmly say "Please". Shouting and chasing was a mugs game, John just found it hilarious and thus it encouraged him to grab more things and run away with them until the excitement was so much that John forgot about the object and it flew out of his hand as he flapped and bounced about with excitement. They'd lost a TV that way only last week when John had managed to put a hard toy through the screen just at the thought that somebody might be about to chase him for it.

John had shrieked with joy and jumped towards him, possibly to push or slap at him as he tried to get around him and run away so he could be chased. The knife, still in John's now flapping hand, had been their contact point and had plunged into Dan's stomach, slightly left of centre and down a bit. Dan had managed to spin as he fell so that he landed on his back and not on top of the knife or on top of John. That much, at least, he had done well. John had shrieked another high pitched giggle at this and then lunged back towards the knife handle, meaning to grab the object of desire once more to continue this game.

In his eagerness to get at the knife John didn't care that he trod on Dan's face but John, at 8 years old now, was already too big and strong for Susan to physically control and getting his shoe in the face was enough of a distraction to cause Dan to make his second mistake. John got hold of the knife handle and pulled at it, it moved and got stuck on something, probably Dan's rib cage. The movement had caused more internal damage; at that point, at the very latest, Dan should have taken control of the knife handle and stopped John from pulling at it again. It could have just been the speed at which John moved, he was very quick something they always pointed out to new carers, or it could have been shock already setting in on Dan; either way Dan failed to react and John was able for a whole second or two to pull and twist at the knife until he got it free and ran off with it. That had been stupid thing number two.

John wasn't stupid and he wasn't without feeling, at some point he would realise Dan wasn't chasing him; he'd lose interest in the knife and drop it. Hopefully that would happen before he bumped into his brother, sister or mother. Hopefully it would happen before he poked it into an electrical socket or hurt himself on it. Dan was hoping John would get back into view soon, so he could at least keep an eye on him, maybe distract him a bit, help kill some time until help arrived. Dan tried to call for John, his voice whispered pathetically. He coughed and tried again; this time it worked and he call out "John!" as cheerfully as he was capable of.

In a neuro-typical brain there are two separate

physical areas for memories of things; one for people, like your mum, a policeman or a stranger you pass on the street, and one for objects, like tables, jam or telephones. In John's brain he just had one area for those things, so they are the same type of thing to him. It meant that he responded emotionally the same way towards a person as he did to a chair. And he expected those objects to respond back to him in the same way. You wouldn't expect a chair not to let you sit on it, or get angry at you if you did; in the same way John wouldn't expect a dinner lady from school not to give him food, so why would it be upset if he hit it when they passed each other in town and it didn't instantly produce food for him.

When John came back into the kitchen he was still happy and he was on the look out for some crisps, he no longer had the knife. Susan would find it a few months later whilst gardening; John had flung it into a patch of high grown weeds in the bottom corner of the garden. Dan had passed out and the flow of liquid from his wound had all but stopped, the kitchen floor was almost covered in it now and the wound was partly plugged by some raw, bloody, sausage looking type thing that had appeared when he'd slumped onto his front as he passed out. John looked at him as he passed the body on his way to the high cupboard that held the crisps. He didn't look at Dan again until after he had climbed up and stood on the kitchen work surface to open the cupboard and get a packet of crisps.

John had to look at Dan then, because one of Dan's functions was opening crisp packets. John had learned this and it had been true for as long as he could remember. Dan wasn't moving. John jumped down from the kitchen work surface but the liquid coming out of Dan covered the whole floor now and John slipped and fell onto his bum. John screamed at the injustice of the floor hurting him and punched at it with his hand that wasn't holding the crisps. Dan still had not moved. John scooted over to him, pausing for only two or five minutes, as drawing patterns in the liquid on the floor distracted him.

It was very interesting, the liquid on the floor. It was a deep dark colour but when John used his finger to draw a line it moved so he could see the kitchen floor and it left bright red edges to his shapes, which were quickly enveloped by the liquid again. He could draw the shape again and again and again and each time the shape would disappear. The dark liquid was interesting to feel too, it was warm and had a slight stickiness. It was very interesting but John really wanted the crisps now. Dan still did not move.

By the time Susan returned home with the other kids John was howling with unhappiness. When she was sad, which lasted a long time after the funeral, she would try to convince herself that the howling had been because John knew there was something wrong with Dan, that he was hurt. That he was dead. She couldn't ever quite shake the thought though, that the howling was mainly just because John couldn't get into the packet of crisps. The crisp packet-opening object had stopped working.

Author's Note

I've changed the names but this is my family, my "John" is actually called Con. Don't worry, my son hasn't killed me, I'm not writing this from the afterlife; but this is one of the scenarios that has gone through both mine and my wife's head. It is something that could happen to us, and the older, bigger and stronger Con gets the more likely it is that something similar to this will happen. Two Christmas's ago Con broke my wife's nose. He didn't mean to and that wasn't what he was trying to do but it is what happened however accidentally it occurred and however unaware of it he was afterwards.

The background stress of the reality of that possibility is just something we've had to get used to and I don't think anybody we know or anybody who works with him really knows or understands that it is there for us. It felt like a good time to let it out. The last sentence almost made me cry (and I'm a big manly man who doesn't do that sort of thing) and after my wife had proof read it for me I saw that she had doodled

"Heart-Breaking" on the back of one page, so I hope it doesn't bum you out too much. It is, after all, still supposed to be a story. For your entertainment.

To be clear though, this is my experience of autism, it will be different than yours however much experience of it you have. More than any other "condition" I know, autism affects each of its sufferers uniquely. Knowing one child or adult diagnosed with autism doesn't give you any more than a small clue about what living with autism in your life is like.

The first sentence of the story came to me a year or more ago and while I knew the general shape of it I didn't know what the story was going to be until I sat down and typed it earlier today. It felt more like writing non-fiction rather than the stories I normally churn out so I'm hoping that I've got the balance of story and information right and it isn't too much of one or the other.

SD

9

Serious stuff. That story was a turning point. The intro and Author's note at the end are 100% true, I've checked up on them. It was his most well received short story and won more than one award actually. Though, like I said, then the world ended and it disappeared.

With its improved writing quality and extensive positive reception SD Downs was encouraged to write full length stories, and whole series of novels. Here is the end of his short story writing days. But the beginning of his novel writing days.

Here's the exciting bit. Having moved into higher land in Scotland, the world as they knew it ended and SD Downs and family were left completely alone. They set themselves up in this house, making a perfect little home of it. Power, water, food, shelter, comfort, they created them all and lived with them for many years.

Inside the house I found a secret room, under the ground floor, built inside of a faraday cage. Look it up, it's how you protect electronic stuff from EMP's. Clever man that SD Downs. I'm guessing that's how I have this working computer here.

In the secret underground protected room I found a small combination lock safe. It took me a few days, but eventually, having worked through many possibly number combinations, I unlocked the safe and found a memory stick wrapped in a note from SD Downs:

Dear Reader,

From when I was very young I had every intention of becoming a novelist, a world wide best seller. I would be rich and famous and I'd write amazing stories. And so I started writing, from that very young age, writing terrible short stories. As I flowed through education and young adulthood I continued to churn out crap.

Then I had to get a job, I married and had children, my life changed, it slowed down and I had less time for my fantasies of becoming an author. Weird thing, it was only then, when I had no time for it, that I noticed when I did write it was no longer complete and utter drivel anymore.

Oh, it still wasn't literary master pieces but through years of practice and maturation I was now capable of writing passable pap that was, if not enjoyable, at least not painful to read. And so, once more I got to it, writing whenever I could.

Every short story that I got published, spurred me on, I won a few short story competitions and eventually I had a literary agent contact me about writing a novel and getting paid for it.

I wrote that novel in less than three weeks, but by the time I had completed it, my first full length novel, the end of the world had begun. For years the world had been falling apart but it waited until I was ready to really start my life before it actually fell.

I survived the end of the world, along with my family, and with nothing else to do I have continued writing my stories with no one left to read them except my family. And now they are gone, and I will join them soon.

If you are reading this, however, then somebody else has survived. I suspect there may be many of us dotted about the place and at some point in the future the Human race will rise again, stronger and hopefully more sensible and smarter. If that is the case then you have found my faraday cage and in it my safe with this note wrapped around a memory stick.

The world's last working computer, as far as I know, should be kicking about here somewhere. Plug the memory stick into it and you'll have access to my life's work. A few hundred novels, all unpublished and unread by anyone but myself, my wife and my kids.

I'd say "Tell me what you think" of them, but if you're reading this, then I'm dead. I'd been intending to find a way to publish them, I even got as far as finding a working printing press on an island not far from here, a town that used to be called Penicuik. But I left it too late, it's too much work for me now. Mayhap you could do that bit for me, reader. Read on…

SD Downs

I found his printing press research, including directions and a map to "Penicuik" from here. The land has probably changed a bit since they were made but I think they should still be followable. If the printing press is still there, and if I can get it to work my intention is to print this as a book and release it to the world. And if that works, if you are reading this in a book held in your hands right now then know that I will be working tirelessly to get everything printed, every single one of his novels and out to you.

Wish me luck

Addendum

I did it! Or at least I think I
have. Getting to Penicuik was a bit
more of an adventure than I thought
it was going to be and getting the
printing press working took a while
not to mention the ordeal of getting
enough paper and ink to work with it
but everything is ready now. You
wouldn't believe what I've had to go
through to get this done, it might
be worthy of a novel of my own.

It's been several years since I
wrote that last "Wish me luck" and
since then I've mainly encountered
bad luck and, as you'll know, there
have been some quite dramatic
changes to the world. Still, here I
am, about to flip the switch and
start the first print run of "Lost
in the Apocalypse" an introduction
to SD Downs, the first book to be
published in a hundred years. The
first of many to come. Hopefully.

Our defences should hold out for a
while but I'm guessing we're going
to need to beef them up a bit, the
noise of the machinery tends to
attract them but if we print during

the day time we should be okay.

I can't put it off any longer. I'm
going to start the presses...

Notes:

Notes:

Notes:

Notes:

Notes:

Notes:

Notes:

Notes:

Simon Downs

SD Downs is only based on me a bit, for a start I'm not dead. The short stories *are* mine (from when I was very young) but the dates and places attached to them have been changed to fit this story. This book is currently self published, I am unconvinced by my choice of fonts and line spacing, any other editorial comments please add in the space provided for notes.

It is true that I once made a Hungarian army officer cry just by speaking to him, in fact, at least half of that list is true. I will let you figure out which half.

Northern Scotland 2020

OMLime

OMLime kindly offered to illustrate the book when their father (Simon Downs) asked them what it was they did all night when they stayed up not sleeping and then were reluctant to go to school in the morning because they were tired. He suspects this may have been a distraction technique but as he liked the drawings so much he hasn't raised it with them again. Much.

OMLime would like it noted that they were only 11 or 12 when they created the pictures in this book and they are over 13 now and a far more accomplished artist than that.